I0744522

# WILD KISSES

*Wilder Irish, book six*

## MARI CARR

Copyright © 2019 by Mari Carr

All rights reserved.

No part of this book may be reproduced in any form or by any electronic or mechanical means, including information storage and retrieval systems, without written permission from the author, except for the use of brief quotations in a book review.

❀ Created with Vellum

# PRAISE FOR WILD KISSES

**"Hot, sexy, romantic and fun,** I loved every moment and this is one I know I'll revisit often." ★ ★ ★ ★ ★ *Slick Reads, Goodreads*

"A **sizzling hot and sweetly emotional** read for the keeper shelf." ★ ★ ★ ★ ★ *Fedora, Goodreads*

"This story was funny, romantic and **tugged at your heart strings**, everything we expect in a book by Mari Carr." ★ ★ ★ ★ ★ *Janet, Goodreads*

"Can your real love be the person you have known pretty much all of your life? **Yes.**" ★ ★ ★ ★ ★ *Mia, Goodreads*

" The stories are extremely well written, poignant, and that bit of light BDSM in most of them just adds that bit of **ZING** that makes them all EXTREMELY WELL **WORTH IT**!!" ★ ★ ★ ★ ★ *Lissa, Goodreads*

"This is my favorite of the Wilder Irish series yet, and **that's saying something.**" ★ ★ ★ ★ ★ *Emma, Goodreads*

PRAISE FOR WILD KISSES

"Another **homerun** for Mari Carr." ★★★★★ *J K, Goodreads*

"*Sigh* What a great, heartfelt story." ★★★★★ *Heather, Goodreads*

*This book is dedicated to my favorite cheerleaders — the Erins.
For their patient guidance, advice, and encouragement
as I rewrote this book 7,249 times.*

# WILD KISSES

*Kiss me once, shame on you. Kiss me twice, shame on me...*

The first kiss with Landon, Sunnie blames on tequila. The second on adrenaline. He did save her and her Louis Vuitton from a mugger, after all.

But then the kiss goes viral and sexy cop Landon is being flooded with female attention. Now it's Sunnie's turn to save Landon—by pretending to be his girlfriend.

It's all fake fun and games and a few orgasms...until Landon's ex comes back to town.

Now Sunnie has to decide if June is just for kisses, or for love and commitment...

# PROLOGUE

"Well, now, lass. Those cookies look just fine." Patrick Collins smiled at his young granddaughter, amused by her impatient expression.

Sunday "Sunnie" Young was no one's fool. She recognized his cookie-baking ploy for exactly what it was. "Can I go play with the boys now?" she pleaded for the eighteenth time in the last hour.

Patrick was hoping the lure of cookies would distract her. "They're playing their video game, sweetheart, and there are only two controllers."

"We can take turns."

Riley had warned him about this. Apparently, Sunnie had become the quintessential annoying little sister in the past few months, constantly begging to play with her older brother, Finn, whenever his best friend, Landon, was around. Riley said they'd been attempting to please both Sunnie, who was desperate to be included, and Finn, who deserved some alone guy time, as much as possible.

Today fell into the "guy time" category.

Riley and Aaron typically managed their schedules so that one of them was available to babysit. And when they couldn't,

Aunt Bubbles was usually able to step in. However, this afternoon, the stars had not aligned. Which meant he was on duty, taking care of the two boys—the Landon sleepover had been planned before Aaron had been called unexpectedly to work at the precinct—as well as Sunnie and baby Darcy.

So far, Darcy had proved to be the easiest of his charges, arriving and remaining asleep throughout the past hour.

He'd been pleased when Aaron had brought Finn's video game console from home and hooked it up before leaving. Aaron had assured Patrick that the game would ensure a relatively easy go of it. And that might have held true if Sunnie hadn't insisted that she wanted to play as well.

They'd already tried the "taking turns" route, and it had ended in a physical struggle as Finn and Sunnie fought over the controller. In order to make peace, he'd suggested the cookie-baking venture. What he hadn't considered was that, of course, the kids would want to eat said cookies. Finn and Landon had already polished off three each with half a gallon of milk.

As the sugar began to kick in, so did the noise level from the living room.

Even that would have been fine.

But that still left him with Sunnie, his precocious, adorable five-year-old granddaughter. Keira had mused only yesterday that perhaps too many members of the family had whammied Riley with that old "I hope you have a daughter just like you someday," and the result had been Sunnie.

She was a whirling dervish of constant motion and chatter and questions and demands. Patrick suspected if there were a way to channel her limitless energy, she could provide enough power in Baltimore for a century.

When she wanted something, she dug in her heels. And right now, she wanted to play with the boys.

Patrick had offered to read her a book, but Sunnie responded to that as if he'd suggested they drown some newborn kitten. Neither sitting still nor listening were her strong suits.

Sunnie gazed longingly toward the boys, her eyes going wide with delight. A glance over the island to the living room proved the increased volume had nothing to do with the game and everything to do with the wrestling match that had started. One Sunnie clearly had every intention of joining.

He raised his hand and said "no" when she started to dart toward the melee.

She stopped, but pouted.

"Boys," Patrick said loudly, in a stern voice. He'd raised four rambunctious boys of his own. Wrestling matches were nothing new to him.

He was pleased when Finn and Landon both looked alarmed, then settled down, quickly apologizing, taking one last swing at each other's arms before starting the video game again.

He turned back to Sunnie, who had somehow snuck out of the kitchen when he'd looked away.

Walking down the hall, he discovered her in his bedroom, jumping on the bed.

"Sit down, Sunnie," he said. "I have an idea." He reached for a photo album he kept on his bookshelf. Opening up the book, he sat on the bed and flipped through a few pages before finding the photo he was looking for.

"That's my mommy," she said, pointing to Riley.

He nodded. "That it is."

"And that's you. You have a lot more hair here. And it's brown, not gray."

Patrick chuckled. "Count how many kids are in that picture, then blame *them* for all the gray hairs."

"Did Mommy make your hair go gray?"

Patrick chuckled, certain at least ninety percent of his gray hairs had Riley's name on them, but he merely shrugged. "I worry about all my kids...so, gray hair."

Sunnie glanced back at the photo. "That's Grandma Sunday, the one I'm named after."

Patrick looked at his beloved wife. Sunday would have

adored this spitfire—and would have had the patience to figure out how to entertain her namesake.

Riley had always been an active little thing as well. He suspected that's why she now served as chef for their family restaurant. Every time Riley acted up, Sunday would pull her into the kitchen and put her to work, patiently answering every single one of her daughter's seventy-two million questions as they cooked. Riley had listened to every word and remembered. Which meant all of Sunday's recipes and baking secrets still lived on.

Sometimes he wondered if Sunday had had a sixth sense about how short her life would be. If she'd somehow known she had to make every moment count. He'd found himself adopting that idea more and more these days, as each year passed and he grew a bit older, slower, and as more grandchildren entered his world. He wanted to pass on pieces of himself—his history and his stories—to all of them.

"Do you know how Grandma Sunday got her name?" Patrick asked.

Sunnie shook her head, her curiosity piqued. "No. Mommy never told me."

Patrick considered that. "I'm not sure your mommy even knows."

"So it's a secret? One only you and me will know?"

He could see she loved the intrigue of that, so he nodded. "It is. Our own secret. Because your name is important and it has a very special meaning."

Her eyes widened and she didn't move. Patrick realized this was the longest he'd even seen her sit still. Even in sleep, Sunnie was a wiggle worm, constantly shifting and shuffling and kicking her covers off.

"You see, it took your grandma a long time to be born, a whole week."

"How long does it usually take?"

Patrick had known there would be countless questions, and

he suddenly regretted where he'd started the story. "Well, that depends. It's different for every baby. It took Teagan three days to be born, but your mommy was born in just a couple of hours. That's not the point of this story," he added quickly. "Let's just say it took her a very long time to be born and it made her mother very tired."

"Mommy was in the hospital with Darcy for two days, but Darcy wasn't in her belly the whole time. Bubbles took me and Finn to McDonald's and ice skating and when we went to the hospital, Darcy was there."

Patrick nodded, grateful Sunnie had a frame of reference that helped her understanding. After all, Darcy was only a few months old, so that memory was a strong one for her big sister. "The whole time your grandma was trying to be born, it rained. Lots and lots of storms. The sky was gray and dreary and everything was wet."

Sunnie crinkled her nose. "I don't like storms."

"Grandma Sunday never liked them either."

"What happened next?"

"The very minute your grandma was born, the rain stopped and the sun came out, bright and beautiful."

"Really?"

Patrick nodded, embellishing the story for her entertainment. "Yes. Her da said it was like magic, like she'd summoned the sun. She'd made it a Sunday, even though it was only Thursday."

Sunnie giggled. "That's silly."

"So when you think about it, your name means you bring sunshine and warmth. You make people happy."

Sunnie smiled, and he could see his words had truly sunk in. She glanced at the picture again. "She's pretty."

Patrick swallowed the lump in his throat her words provoked. "She is indeed."

"When I grow up, I'm going to marry you, Pop Pop, so you won't be alone anymore."

Now he blinked back tears. "That's a lovely gesture, my sweet girl. Would you like to see some more pictures of your grandma?"

Sunnie nodded eagerly, and Patrick was pleased to have found something they could enjoy together. Looking at family photos was one of his favorite things to do.

He flipped the book to the beginning and pointed to the black-and-white photo. "This is my first photo of your grandma Sunday. It's how she looked the year I first met her."

They'd only flipped a few more pages when Landon appeared at the door. "I hurt my elbow."

Patrick spotted the rug burn on the boy's arm. "Wrestling again?"

Landon shrugged, clearly not willing to confess.

"I can fix it." Sunnie darted into the bathroom, emerging with the box of *Toy Story* Band-Aids he kept there. His grandchildren, Sunnie especially, were enamored of Band-Aids, always needing one for some tiny paper cut, scratch or imagined wound.

She peeled off the wrapper, placed the brightly colored bandage on his elbow, and then, adorably, kissed the boo-boo.

Landon smiled in appreciation, then looked at the album in Patrick's hands. "What are you doing?"

"Looking at pictures of my grandma Sunday," Sunnie said. "I'm named after her."

"Can I see?"

Patrick patted the empty spot on the other side of him, and Landon climbed onto the bed as well. They flipped through several pages, as Patrick pointed out who everyone was.

"I'm going to be a Collins one day too," Landon decided, clearly unaware of how families worked.

"You'd make a fine Collins, Landon."

Patrick was even more pleased when Finn found them a few minutes later, hopping on the bed to look at the album as well.

He'd found a way to allow Sunnie to play with the boys with no one complaining.

Patrick wasn't sure how long he and the children sat

there, flipping through the pages as he told them story after story, delighted by their curiosity about his past and their laughter when he told an amusing tale. He was lost in the memories when Riley's voice at the doorway startled him.

"Pop?"

They all looked up together. "Oh, Riley. I didn't hear you come in."

Patrick was amused by Riley's expression—one of confusion and shock.

"What are you doing in here?"

"Looking at old pictures," Sunnie explained. "Of Grandma Sunday and Pop Pop. You made his hair gray."

Riley glanced from her daughter to him and then to the stack of albums on the foot of the bed. They were three deep, but none of the kids wanted him to stop.

"Have you been here a while?"

Patrick glanced at the clock. "About an hour and a half."

Riley's eyes widened. "Hypnosis?"

He gave her a wink. "I'll never tell."

"Aaron got off early. He's on his way back." She looked at the kids. "Grab all your stuff and I'll get the baby ready."

Finn and Landon headed toward the living room, while Riley went to her old room, where the baby was sleeping.

Sunnie stayed behind to help him put the albums back.

"Pop Pop?" she said.

"Yes, lass?"

"I like my name."

He smiled, blinking back unexpected tears. "It suits you, love."

She gave him a hug, repeating her promise to marry him.

He knelt in front of her. "Much as I'd like that, I'm simply too old. So how about another promise?"

She listened intently.

"Promise you'll marry a boy who loves all those things that

make you special, your sunshine and your warmth. Find yourself a boy who appreciates how wonderful you are."

She nodded. "Okay. I promise."

Then he gave her a wink and a grin. "And if you can't find one of those, marry Landon. He has his heart set on being a Collins."

"And the winner of *February Stars*..."

Sunnie could swear every person in the pub was holding their breath, waiting for the announcer to declare a winner. For one month solid, she, her family and the regulars at the pub had gathered around the big-screen TVs to root for their hometown boy, Hunter Maxwell.

"By only twelve votes..."

"Oh my God," Finn yelled at the screen. "Just announce it already!"

Landon caught her eye, winking at her. He and Finn had placed a wager on the competition—Finn putting fifty bucks on Hunter, while Landon remained firmly in Rory Summit's camp.

"The performer who is going to open for The Universe on their worldwide tour is..."

The announcer drew out the word "is" for dramatic effect, producing another curse from Finn. "Where did Les find this tool?"

Les was their aunt Teagan and uncle Sky's band manager, and he'd set up the *February Stars* contest, looking for the "next big act." Hunter had been a last-minute fill-in for one of the performers, and he sure as hell hadn't been expected to last more than the first round. Prior to the competition, he'd really only played with the equivalent of a garage band in his early twenties and, lately, as a pub singer here at Pat's.

"Rory Summit!" the announcer yelled.

Finn groaned as half the pub erupted in cheers, the other half in anger. While Hunter was much beloved at Pat's Pub, his fellow finalist, Rory Summit, had won her way into their hearts as well.

Landon held his hand out, palm up. "Sorry 'bout your bad luck, bro," he teased. "Guess you don't know true musical talent like I do."

Sunnie snorted. "You weren't betting on Rory's talent. You have the hots for her, same as every other guy in here who put money down on her to win."

Landon didn't even bother to deny it. "Maybe. But the fact still remains I now have fifty bucks to woo her with when she shows up later for the after-show celebration."

Finn slapped the cash in his best friend's hand, losing it with zero good grace. "It would take a hell of a lot more than fifty dollars to get her to look at you...especially with *me* here."

Landon and Finn had been friends since preschool, and their constant games of one-upmanship and practical jokes had become the standard operating procedure. Sunnie and Finn's dad, Aaron, had refereed more than his fair share of fights between the two when they were young, when the competitiveness got too heated. Dad claimed the two of them were more like brothers than best friends, and no one had ever disagreed with that assessment.

"Tell your brother he's delusional, Sunshine."

She raised her hands. "Nope. Personally, I think you're both out of your minds if you think someone as talented and cool as Rory would give either of you a second glance. Besides, Landon, you've got a girlfriend."

Landon glanced around the bar, caught Audrey's eye, and waved in a terribly lovestruck, smitten way that had Sunnie rolling her eyes. She pretended she was going to be sick as Finn laughed and picked up on the joke. "I keep trying to figure out what a hot ticket like Audrey sees in Landon."

Typically, Landon would have enjoyed the teasing, would have started giving it right back, but instead, he sobered up. "Audrey's planning to move to New York."

"What?" Sunnie asked. "Since when?"

"She's an actress, you know that. I think it's always been in the back of her mind that she would take the leap, would try to make it on Broadway. I slowed that process down."

"What about you?" Finn asked.

"Audrey wants me to come with her."

Sunnie wasn't sure how to respond to Landon's news. He could have dropped a bomb right in the middle of the pub and it wouldn't have shaken her like this.

Ever since she could remember, it had been her, Finn and Landon. Well, prior to high school graduation, it was more accurate to say it had been Finn and Landon, with her trailing along behind, but that had changed in the past few years.

The idea that their gang of three might drift apart bothered her. There were constants in her life—things she could always count on to be true no matter how old she got. Things like her family's love, a Collins manning the bar at Pat's Pub, her love of Guinness...and Landon's presence.

Those things were solid. Forever.

Finn recovered first. "Are you going?"

Landon shrugged. "I don't know."

"You don't know?" Sunnie asked more hotly than she'd intended. "What about your job?"

When Sunnie considered her unwavering adoration for her family, she figured the only person on the planet who might love them as much—or maybe more—was Landon. She'd seen first-hand the hero worship Landon had developed for her dad. Not that she blamed him, of course. As far as Sunnie was concerned, Aaron Young walked on water. She knew Landon felt the same way.

He'd idolized her dad so much, he had gone to the police academy after graduation, and he now worked as a police officer in the same precinct as Dad. Hell, Dad was his superior officer.

Landon sighed, and Sunnie realized he'd been struggling with this decision for longer than just tonight.

"When did she tell you about the move?"

Landon shrugged. Which meant he didn't want to answer.

She and Finn leaned forward, waiting for the reply.

"Right after the New Year."

"Two months ago? And you didn't tell us?" Finn asked. Sunnie heard the slight tone of hurt in her brother's voice. Finn and Landon were practically brothers, their relationship as tight as Colm and Padraig's, who were legit twins, connected by some sort of invisible thread that meant they were always in each other's heads.

"I don't know what I'm doing yet, Finn."

It was a simple answer, and one she and Finn should have expected. Landon didn't do anything without thinking through every conceivable consequence.

"Let me guess. You have a pros-and-cons list going," Sunnie said, forcing a grin, trying to find a way to ease some of the tension that suddenly hovered over the table.

Landon smirked and started to deny it.

"Don't kid a kidder, babe," she said.

He sighed. "I have a list."

She laughed. "I knew it. What's on it?"

Landon clearly didn't want to tell them. "Just the typical. Pros are new city, new opportunities, Audrey."

Sunnie didn't point out that she thought Audrey probably should have been listed first, but she held her tongue.

"And the cons," Finn prompted.

"Leaving you guys."

She waited for more, but she realized those three words probably encompassed it all. "You guys" meant more than just her and Finn, she knew that. It would include their mom and dad, Pop Pop, her cousins. Landon had been practically adopted into her family when he was just five years old and, like her, he knew that being a Collins meant something—meant everything.

"When is she planning to move?" Finn asked.

Landon looked down at his beer, rather than maintain eye contact with them as he said, "Beginning of March."

"That's next week!" Sunnie said, aghast.

Sunnie looked across the pub again. Audrey and Yvonne were talking to Pop Pop at the bar.

Unlike Landon, there were no dark circles under her eyes, no signs of stress. She'd made up her mind and was looking forward to her future, to trying to make her dreams come true. Meanwhile, Landon was being torn in two.

Sunnie's temper piqued toward the woman. She'd always liked Audrey, always thought she was good for Landon, but that opinion was changing fast.

"When do you have to decide?" Finn asked.

Landon gave him a sad grin. "If I'm going, I have to figure it out this weekend, give Aaron my two weeks' notice on Monday, then pack up my apartment, follow her later in the month."

*If I'm going...*

Sunnie hated the sound of that. Hated the idea of living in Baltimore with one of her brothers—Landon was as good as the real thing—so far away.

As if reading her mind, Landon reached across the table and tapped her hand with his finger—two quick touches to get her attention. "You do realize that New York is only three hours away."

It was far enough away that they wouldn't be sharing Sweet Thursdays together anymore. The concept of Sweet Thursday was created by her uncles Killian and Justin, who'd instituted the tradition of kicking off the weekend one day early by sharing a Thursday happy hour.

It also meant no more weekly Sunday football games together in the Collins Dorm.

That brought up an even more horrifying concern.

"Jesus. You're not going to start rooting for the Giants and the Yankees, are you?" she asked.

Landon visibly winced. "Are you insane?"

They all fell silent, and Sunnie realized there wasn't anything else to say. Landon hadn't made up his mind, and neither she nor Finn would feel right trying to talk him out of it. He was in love with Audrey. They knew that, knew they had no right to stand in his way if his heart chose to follow her.

"You'll call me the second you decide?" Finn asked.

Landon nodded. "Of course I will. I'll call both of you."

Finn cleared his throat, and Sunnie could only assume he had the same lump there that she did. He reached for their empty pitcher and rose. "I'm going to fight my way to the bar for a refill. Don't let anybody take my seat. This place is crazy tonight."

And there was no doubt it would get crazier once the friends and family who'd gone to see the *February Stars* competition live returned from the show.

Sunnie had been delighted by the party atmosphere, ready to dance and drink the night away. Now...

"Don't let this ruin your night, Sunnie. I shouldn't have told you guys here. Truth is, I should have said something way before now. I just...didn't know how. Now it's..."

"Almost March."

Landon nodded. "What do you think I should do?"

Sunnie couldn't help it. She grinned. "Holy shit. You *are* in a bad way if you're asking me for relationship advice."

Landon smiled and rubbed his jaw wearily. "Damn. Good point. This is fucking me up more than I realized. Lost my head there for a second."

She reached across the table and took his hand in hers. "I'll channel Pop Pop for you. He's a better person to talk to about stuff like this. I'm pretty sure he'd say follow your heart."

"Sunnie, that's not—"

"Let me finish. I'm sure it might not feel helpful, but the truth is...it is. This decision is as simple as looking deep inside and figuring out what would make you happiest. Look at Audrey, Landon."

His gaze drifted over to his girlfriend.

"She's doing exactly what I just said. She's following her heart."

"She looks..."

Sunnie saw the moment Landon recognized what she had just seen.

"God, she looks happier than I've ever seen her."

Sunnie nodded. "So make the decision that puts that look on *your* face."

Landon leaned back, and she could tell she'd surprised him. "Wow. Pretty smart, Sunshine." He lifted his pint glass, toasted her, then took a long swig.

"Pop Pop is a very wise man," she joked. "Of course, we could call him over to see if I was right. Maybe even put a wager on it."

He rolled his eyes at her Collins penchant for betting. "That's okay. I'm good. I'm better than good, actually. Thanks for listening, and for...not making that hard. You and Finn are..."

"Spectacular," she filled in when he paused.

However, before he could respond, his attention was drawn to something across the room. She glanced over her shoulder to see what he was looking at.

"Who's the blonde Finn's talking to?" Landon asked, and just like that, it was just another Friday night at the pub, their worries about the future put away in the spirit of enjoying each other's company.

Sunnie stared at the woman for a moment, but decided she'd

never seen her before. "No idea, but he's brushed his hair back off his forehead twice already."

"Oh damn. He's lifting his shirtsleeve, pretending to show her his tattoo when really he's flexing the guns. Mr. Obvious is pulling out all the stops," Landon added.

Sunnie giggled. "What a tool."

"Your brother is turning into a manwhore."

She snorted. "Sort of think he was born that way. Remember the infamous Accidental Two Dates for Homecoming incident?"

"Jesus. Yeah."

During their junior year, Finn had asked a girl to Homecoming during first period. She'd said she wasn't sure she could go because she thought her family was going out of town. Finn had shrugged it off, walked to the back of the classroom and invited another girl, who'd accepted. Five minutes later, the first girl said she'd texted her mom and they weren't vacationing that weekend, and she would love to go with him. Finn had been too embarrassed to tell her he'd already gotten another date after literally a few minutes.

Sunnie had felt like she was trapped in a sitcom for the better part of a week as Finn tried to figure out which girl to let down.

He'd been saved by Landon, who had promised to pick up the pieces. Finn explained the situation to the second girl, who fortunately was more than happy to go to Homecoming with Landon.

"He's gonna have to learn some smoother moves," Sunnie said, turning back to look at Landon.

"I'd say it's a family failing. Something in the genes."

"Excuse me. I'll have you know, Landon Riggs, that my *moves* have moves."

He rolled his eyes. "Come on, Sunnie. I've known you since you were four years old. Remember Joey Dantzler in second grade? Those 'do you like me' letters you used to write him with the yes or no boxes? Those were *really* smooth," he said sarcastically.

She laughed. "I was seven. And the asshole always checked no."

"I haven't noticed you perfecting the art of subtlety since then. How many guys put their number in your phone last weekend at the Power Plant?"

Landon, Audrey, Finn and Sunnie had gone club-hopping on the Inner Harbor the previous weekend.

She crossed her arms. "Three."

"Did you text any of them?"

Sunnie shook her head. "Nope. Decided I wasn't interested."

"Seems to be a theme with you. Dance 'til you drop with a guy, make out during the slow songs, then ditch them at the door."

Sunnie lifted one shoulder casually. "What can I say? I'm young and wild and free."

As if on cue, they broke into the chorus of the Snoop Dogg song in unison, then Sunnie kept going, rapping the Wiz Khalifa part until they started laughing.

"I've got another year of school, and I am in no hurry to fall in love," she said. "Settling down and becoming boring like you is going to have to wait. I have decided to grow up in my thirties."

"Six years is a long time."

She shook her head. "Blink of an eye."

"Not sure I want to meet the guy who convinces you to hang up your hootchie-mama heels."

"He'll be built like John Cena with Chris Pine's eyes, and when we're in bed, he'll—"

Landon cut her off. "Do me a favor, Sunshine."

"What's that?"

"Keep working on that list until what the guy looks like doesn't matter as much as how he treats you."

"*Now* who sounds like Pop Pop?"

He raised one eyebrow until she relented.

"Deal." Then she stood up, leaned forward and gave him a kiss on the cheek. "You're a better brother than my own sometimes."

He lifted one shoulder casually. "You're setting the bar pretty low, but I'll take it."

❧  2  ❧

*year later...*

Landon tossed an empty beer can into the recycling bin and reached into the tub of ice for another.

"Take it easy, cowboy. I'm pretty sure that liquor-to-beer thing only applies if you aren't alternating the two. And you've already done three tequila shots."

He turned and chuckled at Sunnie in her Jasmine costume. She and her cousin Fiona had decided to throw a party on April Fools, giving it an Anything Goes theme. It had come at a time when Landon really needed a distraction. And an excuse to get drunk.

"I'll take my chances."

Sunnie gave him a funny look, tilting her head. "You never take chances. You reason everything out to the nth degree and then do the smart, grown-up thing. It's a very annoying habit of yours. Some might call it a character flaw."

"Well, hold on to your veil, Jasmine, because tonight, I'm all in."

Her eyes lit up. "What's the special occasion?"

"I've been a single man for a whole year."

"Oh, shit. Yeah." Sunnie's gaze softened.

He and Audrey had split up one year ago tonight. Her original plan had been to move to New York in March, but the lease on her first apartment fell through, which left her scrambling to find something else. It also gave her an extra thirty-one days to try to convince him to change his mind and come with her.

It hadn't worked, and since then, Landon had spent countless sleepless nights wondering if he'd made the right decision.

It had been a very long, very heartbroken year, one he was certain he wouldn't have survived without Finn and Sunnie, bolstering him, forcing him to go out and have fun and laugh.

It was funny that all through school, his best friend had been Finn, but since graduation, another name had been given that descriptor as well.

Sunnie, his best friend's little sister. He and Finn had spent the better part of their early school years trying to shake her, the tenacious thing constantly begging to hang out with them.

Shortly after high school, he and Finn both realized how much they liked having her around, and she'd become a part of them, always up for a good time. Sunnie was the epitome of "live in the moment," and she was a lot like her brother—lively, funny, a great storyteller. She was as true a friend as any person could ask for—there to laugh, cry or fight beside you, according to whatever the situation required.

"Is this a drown-your-sorrows night or a turn-the-corner night?" Sunnie asked.

It was a fair question. For twelve months, he'd been as much fun as the proverbial wet blanket. This morning, when he woke up and realized the date, it occurred to him his heart didn't ache anymore. That it hadn't in months, really.

"Turn the corner. We're celebrating."

Sunnie's smile was infectious. "Oh, I can totally get behind that."

And she did. In addition to the bacon feast she'd laid out as their party snacks, she guided them through every drinking game in her repertoire. Then they'd turned on music, alternating between talking and dancing.

Landon hadn't lied about taking his chances. He wasn't a big drinker by nature, but he'd thrown caution to the wind tonight, playing all the games, dancing like a lunatic, his volume matching that of the Collins cousins, which was a feat to be sure.

After getting Flo-Rida "Low," he and Sunnie collapsed on the couch, laughing.

"We should play charades again," Sunnie yelled out to the crowd still dancing in the middle of the living room floor. No one listened. Everyone was too into their own space, enjoying the night.

It had been a wild one, probably one of the best parties he'd ever been to.

"Hey, Sunnie," Landon said, slurring his words slightly, as something just occurred to him. "Where's stunt man?"

"Dumped him a month ago."

"Did I know that?"

Sunnie shrugged. "I dunno. Did it need an announcement?" She was weaving even though they were sitting down, but he wasn't sure if it was her moving or him.

"I guess not."

"You and Finn were right. Couldn't date a guy who dressed like that. I mean what the fuck was up with that jacket?"

"Made him look like a stunt man."

"Made him look like a tool," she countered.

Her Jasmine hairstyle was falling out, the turquoise headband crooked. He reached out to fix it, but wound up making it an even bigger mess until she finally pushed his hand away.

"Are you sure you're okay?" Sunnie asked.

Landon frowned. "No. I'm pretty sure I'm going to have a hangover from hell tomorrow."

She looked at him impatiently. "Not that. I mean about Aub —Audrey." Sunnie stumbled over the name, which Landon found hilarious.

"Of course I am."

"But you're not dating anybody else."

He shrugged. "So?"

"You want me to fix you up?"

"No," he said with more passion than he'd intended. "No Sunnie setups. God only knows—"

"I happen to know a lot of nice nurses from my classes. I think you'd like a couple of 'em. They're just like you. Boring. Looking for love."

He snorted. "That's not a character flaw, Sunshine."

Her face told him she considered it one. The way she crinkled her nose—noses—was adorable. Why did she have two noses?

"I've got this one friend," she continued.

Landon really didn't want to go out on a blind date. Audrey had been a blind date and look how *that* had turned out.

He leaned toward her, capturing her gaze. "You're not listening to me."

Sunnie stopped talking, studying his face. "Yes, I am. I just think that it's time for you to start dating again."

"And you think you know what I want in a woman?"

"Of course I do." She said it with such confidence, such assurance, it annoyed Landon. She always acted like he was an open book—a boring one at that. Landon was the predictable guy, the steady and sure friend who never did anything remotely unusual or interesting.

"You're wrong. You don't have a clue."

His assertion took her aback. For about two seconds.

Then she laughed.

On any other day, at any other time, when Landon was sober, he wouldn't have thought twice about her comments, wouldn't have let them get under his skin.

This wasn't that time.

"I mean it, Sunnie."

His suddenly angry tone seemed to penetrate through the haze of her tequila-fogged brain.

"Landon, listen—"

She was going to argue about it. Of course she was. It was what Sunnie did. For a young woman, she was a dangerous blend of opinionated and confident. It meant winning fights with her took tenacity.

"You don't know a thing about me when it comes to my tastes in women," he assured her.

She started to speak, but he cut her off again when he added, "Or what I like in bed."

That caught her attention. Her eyes narrowed briefly, in shock, then she tilted her head, and he knew he'd piqued her interest.

"Like what?"

He grinned, and the words—freed by tequila and beer and too many nights alone with his hand—came easily.

"I like being in charge in the bedroom, directing everything that happens."

"Like what?" she repeated, stressing the words, wanting more details. She was clearly fascinated.

"I like playing with a woman's breasts, sucking on her nipples until they're hard, bending her over my lap and spanking her ass, tying her up and going down on her, throwing her legs over my shoulders and fucking her like there's no tomorrow...and then flipping her to her stomach and taking her ass the same way."

Sunnie's mouth fell open, and Landon tried to figure out if it was absolute shock or utter horror driving the response.

"Holy shit," she whispered, then she leaned closer, scrutinizing his face. "You're drunk."

He nodded. "So are you."

Their faces were mere inches apart—and that was when it hit Landon.

Hit him like a ton of bricks.

He wanted to kiss her.

He wanted to kiss Sunnie Young.

He'd never in a million years felt that desire, never even considered it.

She was Finn's kid sister, a pain in the ass. To quote her *and* Snoop, too wild, too young, too free. She was the opposite of what he looked for in a woman.

Maybe that explained a lot about his single state.

Jesus. He really *was* drunk.

Time to retreat and revisit this tomorrow without the tequila flowing through his veins.

And he would have done that.

If Sunnie hadn't licked her lips and moved closer.

"Is that really what you like?" she whispered.

He nodded, then Landon met her halfway, his lips touching hers, their tastes identical—the perfect blend of bacon and tequila.

Sunnie kissed like she did everything else in life, with exuberant enthusiasm. Her tongue was in his mouth, her arms wrapping around his neck. He reached for her, his fingers touching her bare midriff, the temptation to move higher to her breasts taunting him.

He was vaguely aware of his surroundings and—

"Sunnie? Landon? What the fuck, man?"

Landon jerked back at the sound of Finn's voice. It took him a second to clear his vision. Sunnie seemed to be struggling to do the same.

Then she moved back, looking adorably confused and... dammit...regretful. *Oops*, she mouthed.

Landon tried to shake off the remnants of the kiss, not wanting to move lest it draw attention to exactly what kind of impact it'd had on him. The fact he was this fucking hard given the level of alcohol in his system was impressive.

Finn was standing next to the couch, glaring down at them. "What the hell was that?"

Sunnie, never one to back down from anything, stood up, flipping her messy hair over her shoulders. "A kiss."

"You two don't kiss."

Sunnie squared her shoulders. "Says who?"

Finn opened his mouth, then shut it. Landon recognized the second his best friend realized he was talking to the wrong person. Finn sat down on the edge of the coffee table.

"Drunk?" he asked Landon, with a surprisingly affable grin.

"As a skunk."

Finn loved the response, as Landon knew he would. With just a few words, he'd assured his friend the kiss wasn't intentional.

It was a mistake.

Or...

Fuck.

It wasn't a mistake.

"Damn, man," Finn said, slapping a hand on Landon's knee. "Not sure I've ever seen you this wasted. Hope you remember this in the morning, because I'm going to have a good time with this story."

Landon rolled his eyes. "I'm sure you will, but for the record..." He decided to prove he could push back just as hard. "I just kissed your sister."

Finn laughed loudly as he stood back up. "Jesus. You're right. The joke's on me. Might have to scratch my own eyes out. That is something I cannot un-see."

Sunnie punched Finn on the arm, calling him an idiot as her brother headed back to the bacon feast.

Landon glanced up at Sunnie, who wasn't very steady on her feet. Part of him considered apologizing to her, but he wasn't sorry. Truth was, he was sorrier Finn had stopped them.

He stood as well.

"That was...interesting," she said, grinning widely, completely unruffled by what had just happened.

Meanwhile, Landon was struggling to keep himself from kissing her again.

She lifted her pinky out to him. "I pinky swear never to ever kiss you again. That was just too freaking weird."

Landon wrapped his pinky with hers, though he made no such vow aloud.

There was nothing *weird* about that kiss.

Nothing at all.

## 3

"Baltimore. There's more than murder here."

Landon nodded as the reporter doing a ride-along with him explained the impetus behind the article he was writing. His superior, Aaron, had already given him the rundown earlier at the precinct. And he'd caught shit from his partner, Miguel, for getting stuck with "babysitting duty."

The phrase that had prompted the New York journalist's story idea was actually a hot-ticket item with tourists—the damn words emblazoned on T-shirts, hats and bumper stickers—sold at nearly every gift shop in the city.

As a cop, working hard to keep Baltimore safe, he took exception to the slogan. In truth, there'd been a decrease in violent crimes last year, but even Landon knew that was hardly something worth bragging about, considering the city still ranked in the top ten when it came to murder.

They continued to drive through the city, Landon making sure to show the man a fair mix of all Baltimore had to offer. There were dangerous areas—that was true of any large city—but there were safer zones as well, places where people could walk without fear.

It had been a long shift, but a glance at the clock in his dashboard proved it was finally over. The reporter hadn't gotten much of a show. They'd answered two domestic violence calls—both involving alcohol—dealt with one mugging, one lost purse, three noise complaints—all in the same neighborhood, thanks to some teens throwing one hell of a wild party in their parents' absence—and issued a handful of citations for driving violations.

"We should probably start heading back. I hope you've gotten enough information for your article," Landon said, turning off Madison, onto a smaller side street. "I realize—"

Landon stopped talking.

As he made the turn, the headlights revealed something for a split second. Dusk had fallen, the tall buildings casting too many dark shadows for him to see much at all. But he was certain he'd seen what looked like two people in a struggle.

Turning on the vehicle's spotlight, he angled his cruiser in that direction.

"What is that?" The reporter pointed through the windshield, sitting up excitedly.

A man was attempting to steal a woman's purse, but she was putting up one hell of a fight.

Landon threw on the flashing lights two seconds after the assailant reacted to the spotlight shining in his direction. The guy shoved the woman roughly to the ground and took off running.

"Stay here," he ordered the reporter, getting out of the car. Landon unfastened his gun, a protective measure in case the man came back. Using the walkie-talkie on his shoulder, he requested backup and reported his location.

The woman was pushing herself up when he approached.

He was less than ten feet away when he recognized the dark blonde hair.

"*Sunnie?*" He raced to where she sat, kneeling next to her. The spotlight from the car was bright, both of them squinting. It took a second for his eyes to adjust to the sudden light.

She looked up at him, and he saw the determination in her

eyes. There was a red mark on her cheek that was probably going to turn into a nasty bruise.

Landon glanced around the surrounding area. The man was long gone. "Are you okay?"

She was still wearing her nurse's scrubs, but he couldn't understand how she'd gotten from Johns Hopkins to here. Surely she wasn't walking home at this time of day? It was a three-mile trek and it was nearly dark.

Sunnie nodded. "Yeah. I think so. Son of a bitch was trying to steal my purse."

"And you thought fighting back was a good idea?" He touched the red mark on her cheek. Landon's temper sparked as he considered what could have happened to her.

She tilted her head, as if he'd missed the most important part. "He was taking my *purse*, Landon."

"So?"

"So...it's a Louis Vuitton. I love this purse."

He shook his head. "Are you serious right now?"

She brushed off his concern. "The guy wasn't even that big, and I'm pretty sure I was winning."

Landon looked at the mark on her face and lost his shit. "Who gives a *fuck* how big he was? Do you understand how stupid and dangerous it is to fight back? He could have had a weapon or—"

"Okay," she said hastily, simply to stop his tirade. "Okay. I'm sorry. Really. But..."

Here we go.

Sunnie was the queen of "buts."

She lifted the bag. "It's a new purse, my gift to myself for graduating and getting the nursing job at the hospital. It was super expensive. And it's *mine*," she stressed.

"I don't care how much it cost! You could have been seriously hurt!"

"I know." Then she gave him her standard Sunnie grin, the one that told him he wasn't going to like what she said next. "I don't suppose we could keep this to ourselves and not tell anyone about it?"

By anyone, she meant her dad.

"We need to file a report."

She considered that. "Yeah, but he didn't actually get my bag. And I'm not hurt. Honest."

He tried to do a visual inspection of her. They were kneeling on the ground. He couldn't see any cuts or blood, and her clothing was still intact, just the red mark on her cheek.

She was the picture of calm, cool and collected, even after the battle she'd just waged. Meanwhile, his heart was racing a million miles a minute as he imagined everything that could have happened.

He tried to lock it down, even as he pulled her into his arms, hugging her tightly. "Jesus, Sunshine," he murmured.

Sunnie accepted the hug, though he could tell she was surprised at first. "I really am sorry, Landon. Swear to God, next time," she murmured against his chest, "I'll let go of the bag."

He wasn't sure who was comforting whom with the hug. He sort of thought she was trying to calm him down. The problem was, he knew all too well how badly things could have gone. Then he realized she was trembling slightly.

Ah, so she *did* get it. He tightened his hold.

"What were you doing out here alone?"

She pushed away to face him. "Derek picked me up after work. We got into a fight. I told him to go fuck himself, and the asshole stopped the car and told me to get out. I should have stayed on the main street, should have called for an Uber, but I was pissed off. I stormed away and then...that guy jumped me, and I kind of went all Tasmanian Devil on his ass. Guys suck."

Sunnie was impulsive. She acted on emotion—*reacted*—then considered the consequences later.

"He made you get out? Here?" he asked, glancing around the dark street. Derek, the latest in a long line of occasional boyfriends, had dropped her off in the middle of a sketchy neighborhood. "I'm going to kill that motherfucker," he muttered.

His words had come out more serious, more deadly than he'd intended. The tone obviously caught Sunnie by surprise yet again.

She looked up at his face and laughed. "Wow. Dial it back a notch, Landon. That Rambo thing is a serious turn-on."

He closed his eyes, praying for patience…and to calm down. He hadn't quite forgiven her for being so reckless.

They really were polar opposites, always had been. Sunnie had personality to spare, while Landon was the quiet one. Calm, stoic. If she was the queen of overreaction, he was lord and master of composed. This time, the roles felt reversed.

He stood up, helping her rise as well. She winced slightly, leaning heavily on him.

"What the hell?" he asked, looking down.

She grimaced. "Okay, well, now, don't get pissed again…but I appear to have twisted my ankle."

"I'm taking you to the hospital."

She shot him an incredulous look. "I'll get laughed out of the E.R. if I show up asking them to take care of something this silly! It's fine."

"Sunnie," he started to insist.

"I'm a nurse, Landon. Trust me."

She'd graduated from college a month earlier, jumping right into work from her residency after wowing the doctors and her professors. She was a born caregiver, her humor and bedside manner making her the perfect nurse.

A year ago, she'd expressed an interest in pursuing oncology nursing after serving as a bridesmaid in her cousin Padraig's wedding. Padraig had married a beautiful woman named Mia, who'd died a few months after the ceremony.

Sunnie had always lived life with wild abandon. However, after Mia died, she took the pursuit of her career, the way she wanted to help others, more seriously.

What she hadn't managed to tone down was her party-girl image, the way she spent her free time with losers like Derek.

"Okay. No hospital. But we really do need to go to the precinct, file a report."

"Hell no."

He raised an eyebrow.

"Please don't make me. Dad will kill me."

He shrugged. "That doesn't sound so bad to me. After the stunt you just pulled." It was clear he hadn't made much headway on showing her the error of her ways. Maybe Aaron could.

"Please, Landon! Can't we just keep this between ourselves? There's no reason to upset everyone." He noticed her hands were shaking, and it suddenly occurred to him that as the adrenaline wore off, she *was* starting to get it.

"Sunnie, what you did was reckless."

She leaned closer, batting her big blue eyes at him. If she were a stranger, he might have been charmed. But this was Sunnie, and he knew all her tricks when it came to getting her way. "Do you mind just taking me home?"

It was against procedure. A crime had been committed. A report needed to be filed, questions needed to be answered. They needed a description of the assailant. Landon was a rule follower. He always had been.

"Sunnie," he started again.

"Landon," she cooed.

"You realize that will never work with me, right?"

She straightened up, the fake sweetness evaporating, the real Sunnie emerging. Funny how he preferred the sass over the sugar. "Oh my God. I have had the shittiest night in history. Please, don't play Boy Scout tonight."

Her words tweaked his temper. Sunnie constantly cast him in the eternal do-gooder role, while throwing herself at bad boy after bad boy.

She'd avoided him since that kiss on April Fools. He hadn't

realized it until this minute, but when he considered the last two months, he saw the truth.

He'd let her get away with it because he had been fighting his feelings for her, trying to convince himself his memory of that kiss was too clouded by tequila to mean anything.

"I swear this is only going two ways, babe," she insisted. "I can ride in the cruiser with you back to the pub. Or walk home on my shitty ankle. Either way, there is no way I'm going to the pre—"

"Goddammit, Sunnie!" Landon cupped her cheeks, leaned forward and kissed her. Just to shut her up.

Sunnie jerked slightly, shocked by his impulsiveness. Then her lips softened against his, her head turning ever so slightly as she pressed closer. He opened his mouth and she opened hers, their tongues touching. Her hands rested against his chest, his bulletproof vest preventing him from feeling them there.

He wanted them against his bare chest, wanted her to feel how hard his heart was beating...for her.

Jesus.

For her.

Sunnie broke the union first. One look at her face proved she didn't understand what had just happened any more than he did.

He was the thinker. She was the doer.

But tonight...he flipped the roles, acting on instinct.

"What the hell was that?"

"I was trying to shut you up," he lied, struggling to pull himself together.

She laughed. "Well, I guess that's one way to do it. You also could have told me to stop talking."

He snorted. "Like that would work."

The look she gave him proved she knew he was right and agreed.

Regret was setting in. Not over the kiss itself—that had done things to his libido he didn't want to consider, just like it had at the party.

But once again, his timing sucked.

The first kiss happened when they were wasted. Now this one coming right on the heels of an attempted mugging.

He needed to figure out what the hell was going on with him in regards to Sunnie—and quick.

"I really am sorry," she whispered.

It was a sincere apology, so he nodded and accepted it.

"Forget it. And the kiss."

Unfortunately, that request reminded her of the first kiss. "Didn't we already do that...a couple of months ago?"

He nodded. "Yeah. Maybe we can wash this one away with a few too many shots of tequila too. I could use a drink right about now."

The April Fools party two months earlier was turning out to be one of those parties everyone would talk about for decades, remembering how, for just one evening, every single person in the room had been in the perfect mood to cut loose and go wild.

Finn was still having a great deal of fun at Landon's expense, teasing him about how drunk he'd gotten. No doubt Finn had latched on to it because it was such a rarity. Nine times out of ten, Landon was the designated driver. That night, he'd just wanted to kick back and have fun.

The one thing Finn didn't mention was the kiss.

When Yvonne mentioned it the next day, Sunnie had been shocked, thinking her cousin was joking. That was when Landon realized Sunnie didn't remember kissing him, so he decided to make things a lot easier for both of them by pretending the same.

But things *had* changed between him and Sunnie after that party.

For him, anyway. Ever since that night, it was like he was seeing her through different eyes.

Sunnie took it in stride, like she did everything—including *this* kiss—and she'd started dating Derek the Douchebag the next week. Sunnie had jumped into her relationship with Derek like every other one in her life, all in…for one hot minute.

"At least there weren't any witnesses this time," she said, her smile growing brighter.

"We got lucky. None of your cousins or your brother around to give us shit."

He clipped the latch on his gun holster, looking toward the end of the street at the sound of approaching sirens.

"You called for backup?"

"Of course I did."

"Shit," she murmured, aware it was going to be impossible to keep this from her dad once the other guys from the precinct arrived.

Landon looked at her…and couldn't stop thinking about the kiss. And the fact that he wanted to do it again. She looked back, her eyes curious.

Then her gaze dropped to his lips.

She wanted to kiss him again too.

For a moment, Landon considered giving in to that desire, but the sirens were too close.

"We need to talk, Sunshine," he said, using the nickname he'd been using since they were kids. It had started as a way to tease her because she always got annoyed, claiming her name was Sunday, not Sunshine, but eventually the complaints fell away and the name stuck.

Sunnie nodded, her face growing more serious. "I know. I really am sorry, Landon. What I did was stupid and dangerous."

She mistakenly thought he wanted to talk about her actions.

She was wrong.

The only thing he intended to discuss were *his* actions.

And his feelings regarding those kisses.

## 4

Sunnie started to walk to the police car, but her pained limp was too much for Landon to watch. He bent down and picked her up, despite her protests, carrying her to his cruiser and setting her down gently to lean against the vehicle as two police cars roared into view.

"Stay here. I'll see if I can...do some sort of damage control.'"

She gave him a quick kiss on the cheek. "Thanks, babe."

Landon filled the other officers in on what had happened as Sunnie waited by his car with the reporter. He'd completely forgotten about the other guy until Landon had carried her back to the vehicle and seen him watching them. So much for no witnesses. At least this one wasn't a Collins.

The four other officers planned to search the area for the mugger, though Landon didn't hold out much hope that they'd find anything. The guy was long gone.

He was halfway to the pub, after dropping the reporter off at the precinct parking lot to grab his own car, when Aaron's voice came over dispatch.

"Where's my daughter, Officer Riggs?"

"Dammit," Sunnie muttered from the passenger's seat.

Landon picked up the handheld, speaking into it. "She's with me, Lieutenant."

"And where are you?"

Landon glanced over at Sunnie. "Taking her home."

There was a moment of silence over the radio. Then Landon's cell phone rang, Aaron's name appearing on the screen.

Sunnie rolled her eyes.

"Yes, sir," Landon said as he answered it.

"I want to see my daughter."

"I know, sir. But she wanted to go home. I promise you she's fi—"

"She needs to file a police report, Landon."

"I know that, sir, but she wanted—"

"Dammit, Landon! Stop with that 'sir' shit. There are protocols that need to be followed, and I want to see my daughter. Want to know that she's okay. Then I want to shake some everloving sense into her. What the hell happened?!"

"A guy tried to steal her purse."

"And?"

Landon wasn't sure how to respond to that. Sunnie was going to have a bruise on her cheek tomorrow and she was limping. It was going to be obvious she put up a fight, which would send Aaron into orbit. "And, um—"

"Give me the phone," Sunnie said, holding out her hand. Landon hesitated, then decided this was his chance to get out of the middle.

She took the cell phone. "Dad, listen—"

There was a pause, and Landon could only assume Aaron was reading her the riot act.

"I'm fine. I will come down first thing in the morning to file the damn complaint. Even though that seems pointless. The guy didn't get—"

There was silence...a long silence.

Sunnie sighed. "Who told you I put up a fight?"

*Uh-oh.*

She gave him a look and mouthed the word *reporter*.

Then she sighed as she turned to look out the passenger window. "I know it was stup—" Aaron didn't appear to be in the mood to listen to her excuses. "I know, but—" He kept cutting her off. "Yes, but—"

Landon considered what he'd seen of the fight. The dude *had* been bigger than Sunnie, and he hadn't been messing around. It was obvious he'd intended to keep going until he got the purse, and God only knew what he would have escalated to if she'd kept holding on to it.

Landon glanced over at the mark on her cheek. He couldn't tell if it was the result of a punch or a slap. His chest seized at the thought, his grip on the steering wheel tightening until his knuckles went white.

"Please hold Mom and Bubbles back. They can yell at me tomorrow. I'm going home. Landon's with me. I know everyone is worried...and, okay, pissed off, but please, Dad, call off the dogs tonight. I worked a ten-hour shift, broke up with Derek, got my ass chewed out by Landon *and* you. I will see you first thing in the morning and give you a chance to do it again in person. Promise."

Her plea must have worked. "Thanks, Dad. I love you too. Here," Sunnie said, handing the phone back to him. "Dad wants to talk to you again."

"Aaron," Landon said to let him know he had the phone back.

"Walk her into the pub and all the way upstairs to the apartment. Don't leave there until you know she's okay—and I don't just mean physically. The reporter told me she took a hit and a hard shove to the ground. She might talk a good game, but I can tell she's shaken up, and what could have happened is going to sink in soon. Finn was at the Orioles game. I finally got ahold of him and he's on his way home. Yvonne and Padraig are downstairs at the pub. Stay with her until Finn gets there."

"Yes, sir."

"And, son," the emotion was thick in Aaron's voice when he continued, "thank you for taking care of my little girl tonight."

"I didn't—"

"Yes, you did. I'll talk to you in the morning. Goodbye, Landon."

The call disconnected just as they arrived at the pub. Landon parked the cruiser, then walked around the car and wrapped his arm around her waist, allowing her to lean on him as she walked slowly, careful not to put too much weight on her ankle.

"Sunnie. I wish you would let me—"

Before he could repeat his request to take her to the hospital, she shook her head. "Elevation, Advil, and ice. It'll be fine by morning."

Landon could only assume Aaron had texted her family about what had happened, because Padraig and Yvonne were there to greet her with hugs. Along with more than a few, "What the hell were you thinking's" from Paddy, while Yvonne whispered, "At least you saved the purse."

Sunnie broke away after a few minutes, and he noticed she was starting to look tired. He helped her upstairs.

"Finn will be home soon."

Sunnie nodded, her steps slowing as they reached the apartment. Whatever strength she'd had left had been expended on the phone call and the walk upstairs. She dropped down on the couch, her elbows on her knees, her face in her hands.

"Sunnie?"

"I've never been hit before. It hurt." Then she gave him a regretful look. "I should have given him the purse. I was just so pissed off at Derek. I struck out without thinking, you know?"

He nodded, and then sat next to her, pulling her toward him until her face rested against his shoulder.

Neither of them spoke as they let the night play out in their minds. Landon couldn't stop thinking of all the things that could have happened, his terror growing more and more until he thought he'd explode.

He gripped her tighter, afraid he might be hurting her, until she matched his strength, her arms a vise around his waist. He wasn't sure how long they remained that way, just holding each other.

She fell so silent, he thought perhaps she'd fallen asleep.

Then he heard Finn's footsteps on the stairs. Her brother was coming up fast, taking them two at a time.

Sunnie's head lifted from his shoulder as Finn entered, kneeling in front of her.

"Jesus, Sun. Are you okay?"

She nodded as Finn brushed the back of his knuckles gently over the coming bruise, his eyes dark with anger.

"The fucker *hit* you?" Finn was the textbook description of an overprotective brother.

Landon recalled the night of their junior prom. A guy in their class had asked Sunnie to the dance. He wasn't someone they hung around with, but he was a decent guy. Even so, Sunnie had only been a sophomore, and Finn had insisted she and her date go to dinner with him, Landon, their dates, and two other couples.

Landon and the other guys had stopped by to pick up Finn and Sunnie in the limo before going to get the other girls. Finn had come downstairs first, and he raised a threatening finger in their faces, saying, "I don't want to hear one word about my sister."

Landon had looked at one of the other boys, both of them confused—until Sunnie walked in. She'd worn a skintight, shimmery aqua dress that had hugged her newfound curves like it had been custom-made for her and reminded Landon of a mermaid —the sexiest mermaid in the history of the world. Her blonde hair, typically pulled back in a braid, had been loose and wavy over her bare shoulders. She wore makeup, her eyes accentuated by mascara and her lips shiny with pink gloss.

Landon hadn't considered Sunnie a girl until that moment.

He and the other guys stared, their mouths hanging open.

Landon had started to say something, started to tell Sunnie she was the most beautiful girl he'd ever seen, but Finn stepped in front of him, blocking his view.

"Not. One. Word."

Finn's big-brother growl had broken the spell and Landon had laughed, giving Sunnie, who'd been in her element, a wink.

Finn ran a hand through his hair, drawing attention to his hat head. He'd lost his Orioles cap somewhere in the mad dash home.

Sunnie took Finn's hand and squeezed. "Please don't freak out, Finn. I swear I'm okay. Honest."

"What were you doing walking home alone? I thought Derek was picking you up. Where the hell was he? Didn't the two of you have plans for tonight?" Finn asked, firing off question after question without giving her a chance to answer.

"He's a dick. I'm over him."

Finn shook his head and sighed. "You gotta stop dating douchebags, Sun."

She laughed. "You know they don't start out douchebags, right?"

He narrowed his eyes.

"Fine," she said, raising her hands. "Derek was a douchebag pretty much from the beginning. I just feel like the dating pool in Baltimore is getting smaller. It's really tough to find—"

"Don't change the subject," Finn grumbled. "Did you seriously fight to keep the purse?"

Sunnie huffed. "It was my new purse."

Finn stood up, clearly intent on repeating the same thing Landon and Aaron had said.

She rose as well, the two of them practically standing nose to nose, as much as they could considering Finn was a good eight inches taller.

"I love that purse," she insisted.

Landon knew exactly how this was going to end. Sunnie was getting tired of being lectured to, which was going to make her contrary. She was a master button-pusher. Given what she'd been through, and the fact she'd genuinely apologized to him, Landon figured they didn't need to keep piling on.

Unfortunately, Finn was in annoyed-big-brother mode and getting ready to really dig in.

Finn moved closer. "I swear to God, Sun, I can't bel—"

"It *is* a great purse," Landon said, stopping both of them in their tracks, as he stood and stepped between them.

Finn looked ready to kill him, but that was countered by Sunnie's genuine laugh when Landon continued, "It's a Louis Vuitton, man. Have a little respect."

"Finally, someone who appreciates my efforts." Sunnie stifled a yawn and Landon spotted the weariness in her eyes that said she'd had enough. "You can get in line behind Mom, Dad and Bubbles to give me shit tomorrow, Finn. I'm really tired tonight."

Finn looked like he wanted to press on, but Landon shook his head subtly.

"Okay," Finn begrudgingly agreed. "It can wait. You sure—"

"I'm fine," she repeated.

Landon was touched when she gave him a quick kiss on the cheek. "Thanks for everything, Landon. I'm going to bed."

Finn moved over to allow her to pass, his brows furrowing when he saw her limp.

Landon reached out to grab Finn's arm, to keep him from asking her about it. His silent request gained him a scowl, but he and Finn were best friends, closer than brothers, so he followed Landon's lead.

When she was gone, Finn turned to him for all the answers Sunnie wouldn't provide.

"Where was Derek?" he asked.

"They broke up. It turned into a fight and the asshole kicked her out of the car."

"I'm going to fucking kill him," Finn muttered.

"Get in line. I'm at the front of that one."

"What's wrong with her ankle?"

Landon shrugged. "Dude shoved her down, but she wouldn't let me take her to the hospital. She says it's just twisted and that it'll be fine by morning. She played the 'I'm a nurse' card."

"How much did you see? That guy who grabbed her...?"

Landon saw very little beyond the struggle. "I didn't get a good look at him. It was dusk. I saw most of it through the dimness outside and the headlights of my cruiser. It happened pretty fast."

At least, *his* part did. The guy saw the cop car and panicked, ran off. He didn't know how long Sunnie had been struggling, and he'd missed seeing the guy hit her.

"You going back to the precinct?" Finn asked.

Landon shook his head. "No, I was at the end of my shift when..." He didn't finish the sentence, exhaustion kicking in for him too. It had been a long night.

"You headed home?" Finn asked.

Landon nodded slowly, glancing down the hallway toward Sunnie's room. He didn't want to go home, wasn't sure he could leave her alone yet. As long as he was close, he could protect her. Which was ridiculous. There was no threat.

"You wanna stay here?" Finn asked.

"Yeah. I do."

Finn had an extra bed in his room that belonged to his cousin Fergus when he was home on leave, which was rarely. As a result, Landon always had a place to crash after a few beers in the pub with the Collins clan.

Finn turned on the television, searching for the Orioles game he'd just left. It had gone into extra innings. Then he grabbed them both a beer from the kitchen. "I need a distraction," Finn said. "If I sit here and think about her wrestling for... Goddammit, the guy could have had a weapon, could have really hurt her!"

"Don't think about it," Landon said. He was obsessing over it enough for both of them.

He and Finn sat quietly, watching the game, sipping their

beer. Landon was fairly certain neither of them was paying much attention to it, but he was glad for the chance to be near Sunnie.

The game ended, but they still didn't move, just kept watching the wrap-up sportscast and then the nightly news. It was well after midnight when Finn stood up and announced he was going to bed. Yvonne had come in a few minutes earlier, chatting before heading back to her own room next to Sunnie's.

Landon wondered if Sunnie had managed to fall asleep, or if, like him, she was struggling to shut her thoughts down.

"Come on, man," Finn said. "You don't need to guard the door."

Landon stood up slowly. He'd debated all night about whether he should tell Finn about the kiss. In the end, he had decided not to. The kiss had been impulsive, ill-timed, and something Sunnie appeared to want to forget.

Landon should probably do the same. But he wasn't going to. He couldn't.

"Okay."

Finn remained at the foot of the stairs that led to the landing outside his attic bedroom. "You saved her."

Landon shook his head, but Finn wouldn't let him shrug off what he'd done.

"You were there. You saved her. I'm never going to forget that, brother."

His peace spoken, Finn climbed the stairs.

Landon was slower to follow.

He'd spent most of his childhood wishing he'd been born into this family, a brother, a cousin, a son.

Landon adored his mother, but without a father or siblings of his own, he'd reached out and grabbed hold of Finn and Aaron, Darcy...and Sunnie.

Tonight, Aaron had called him son. And Finn, brother.

Those words felt like a dream come true.

Until he considered Sunnie...and that kiss.

❧   5   ❧

Sunnie trudged down the hallway toward the kitchen, rubbing her eyes. They felt gritty and dry from too little sleep. She'd heard Yvonne get up about an hour earlier, knew her cousin had peeked into Sunnie's room to check on her, but she'd pretended to still be asleep, unwilling to deal with everyone giving her hell for last night. At the moment, Landon appeared to be the only one who'd forgiven her stupidity. Which only left seven hundred and thirty-seven Collins family members to go.

When she entered the kitchen, it was close to noon. She was surprised to find not only Yvonne and Finn there, but her sister, Darcy, as well. Typically when there were three or more of her family members in a room, the noise rose to ungodly levels. Hell, even their whispers were loud.

This morning, they were silent, and until she saw all of them there, she'd thought everyone had headed out for the day and she was alone in the apartment.

They turned to look at her, and she prepared for the onslaught.

"Wow," she said sardonically. "Sort of disappointed by the turnout. Only three of you here to lecture me?" she asked.

"Couldn't get Fergus home from overseas? Fiona over from California?"

Yvonne laughed. "We thought we'd take it in shifts. Landon's grabbing a quick shower and there are quite a few others waiting downstairs in the pub."

"Landon spent the night," Finn said. "He was worried about you."

She waited for him to say more, wondering if Landon had confessed about the kiss. When Finn didn't say anything about it, she knew Landon had kept that tidbit to himself.

"Okay," she replied, shrugging one shoulder casually. Landon stayed over two or three nights a month. Given everything that had happened last night, she wasn't surprised he'd wanted to stay close. His cop instincts had been working overtime.

If she was being completely honest, she was glad he was still there. She wasn't sure why, but with him around, she felt...

She felt horny.

Which was the completely wrong emotion—was horniness an emotion?—for this situation.

Finn still looked miffed, and she knew he had every reason to be angry. She had put herself in danger. However, she had to admit she was a bit surprised by the level of his anger at the moment. Finn, like Landon, was usually very good at letting things slide off his back.

"Landon told me why you were on that street alone. Please stop dating shitheads, Sunnie."

Then she realized Finn was in bulldog mode and not ready to settle down over Derek dropping her off in a sketchy area.

In truth, she'd already forgotten about Derek, too distracted by Landon's kiss to give a shit about the ex-boyfriend.

She took a deep breath, smiling at Darcy. "I guess Dad's probably losing his shit. I'd promised to go in this morning and make a statement." She was in her pajamas and dreading the thought of going to the precinct. As if she didn't have enough overprotective males in her family, she figured that number was easily doubled when she added in her dad's fellow cops, a lot of whom she'd known for most of her life.

Maybe she could talk Darcy into going with her. Darcy was bubbly, sweet and adorable. They could stop off for a couple dozen doughnuts, then go in and try to buy their dad's forgiveness with sweets.

Darcy shook her head. "No need to bother. Dad called a little while ago. Said Landon could just take your statement here."

Finn poured a glass of orange juice and handed it to her, then poured one for himself.

"Cool," she said. At least Landon had calmed down, unlike her brother. It would be easy to talk to him about what had happened because he'd seen most of it.

As if summoned, Landon appeared in the kitchen, his hair wet from the shower. He'd borrowed jeans and a T-shirt from Finn. Sunnie recognized Finn's beloved retro Van Halen shirt.

"Hey, Sunshine. You slept late."

"Yeah, I did."

They heard voices coming from the stairs, and Sunnie sighed.

"They've been downstairs in the pub since eight o'clock this morning," Finn told her as the sound of her mom and Bubbles's loud voices drifted to them from the living room. "I told them you needed the sleep."

"Thanks," she murmured to her brother mere seconds before Mom walked into the kitchen, crossing the room to pull her into a big hug.

"I'm okay, Mom," Sunnie said, wondering if that statement would hold true when Bubbles engulfed her from behind, the two women squeezing her with the combined strength of a boa constrictor. "Um...I can't breathe."

"Hush," Bubbles said, clenching even tighter. "I swear to God, Riley and I both lost ten years off our lives last night when your dad told us what happened."

Mom released her first. "Finn said Derek left you alone on the street."

"We had a fight. I broke things off. Probably should have waited to tell him what an asshole he was until I was closer to home." It was a weak-hearted attempt at a joke, but Sunnie was struggling to find her footing.

She and Derek were hardly a serious item. They'd gone out half a dozen times in the past month or two, and she hadn't even slept with the guy because...she just hadn't been feeling it.

"I'm going to kill that son of a bitch," Bubbles declared menacingly.

Finn and Landon said in unison, "Get in line."

"This isn't really Derek's fault. I should have found a café and called an Uber. Instead, I was pissed off and started walking, even though it was getting dark. It was a really stupid thing to do."

"Damn right it was. Child, your mother and me did not raise you to act like a damn fool," Bubbles said.

Sunnie laughed. She adored her "aunt" Bubbles. Loved the woman's straight-shooting ways, her foul language and her extremely inappropriate stories about when she was a 'ho back in Vegas.

Mom shook her head. "Don't take up for the man, Sunnie. A nice guy would have driven you home no matter what. I think Bubbles and I might pay him a visit and educate him about that."

Sunnie suspected Derek might prefer an ass-whooping from Finn and Landon over a tongue-lashing from Bubbles and Mom, but she didn't bother to try to talk her mom out of it. It would be a pointless battle to wage. Riley Young protected her children more fiercely than a lioness. She'd give Derek a piece of her mind, no matter what Sunnie said.

"I'm fine," Sunnie stressed. "Honest." Then she looked at Landon, anxious for a chance to escape them. "Finn said you're supposed to take my statement."

He nodded.

"Not yet," Mom said. "There's someone else waiting to talk to you."

"Who?"

Mom pointed down. "Pop's in the pub. He's fretting and won't feel a moment's peace until he sees you. Go talk to him."

Sunnie wasted no time, racing back to her room to don a pair of jeans and a T-shirt. She threw her hair up in a ponytail, thinking it was good enough. Then she glanced in the mirror—and spotted the baseball-sized bruise on her cheek.

There was no way she'd let Pop Pop see that.

Grabbing some foundation and powder, she did her best to conceal it, then headed downstairs.

Pop Pop was sitting at his usual place at the bar. It was lunchtime, so there weren't more than a dozen or so folks scattered around the pub, grabbing an early afternoon drink. Sunday's Side, the restaurant, was busier with the lunch rush.

He smiled when he saw her, but the expression didn't reach his eyes. She walked straight into his outstretched arms.

"I'm okay, Pop Pop," she whispered to her beloved grandfather.

"Lie to the others all you want, lass. But you don't have to say those words on my account. I know you're not. Just sit here and stop pretending so hard."

"You're not going to yell at me too?" she asked.

Pop Pop shook his head. "I suspect Aaron, Finn, and Landon have handled that well enough."

She giggled. "You forgot Mom and Bubbles."

"So we'll skip the lecture and move on to the feelings. How are you feeling?"

"I..." She wasn't sure what to say. When the guy first grabbed for her purse, she was furious at Derek, pissed beyond belief and, honestly, sort of looking for a fight. She'd spun around swinging, taking the guy by surprise—for a split second. They'd both kept hold of the purse strap, doing some silly tug-of-war over it for a few seconds before he swung at her, the back of his closed hand striking her cheek with enough force that she saw stars.

And yet she still wouldn't let go of the purse. She had no idea what the guy would have done next because that was when Landon showed up, the police lights scaring the guy off. He'd let go of the bag, shoving her down as he took off in the opposite direction. Off-balance, she'd twisted her ankle on the way down.

At least she'd been right about one thing last night. Her ankle was much better this morning, stiff but not sore.

"You what?" Pop Pop prompted when she didn't respond right away, reclaiming his seat and patting the one next to him.

She shrugged as she sat down.

"Should I take a stab at it?" he asked.

She smiled and nodded.

"You're scared. No, I wager you're terrified out of your wits, now that you've had some time to think about it all. You're upset about putting yourself in danger—walking alone and fighting back. You're a smart girl who's feeling stupid for believing her beloved hometown could hold such evil people."

Most of his assessment was true, which only made her feel even dumber. "We live in Baltimore, Pop Pop. My dad is a cop. I have no illusions about what's lurking out there."

"Yet it's never touched you. And that gave you a sense of misguided security."

She nodded. That was definitely true. Sunnie had lived in a bubble of safety and love, surrounded by Collins men and her father's police buddies.

"You've also never been hit. That will take you some time to bounce back from. You need to give yourself that time. Don't pretend for my sake or anyone else's."

As always, Pop Pop gave the best advice.

Before they could say more, Dad entered the pub. He walked directly to her, tugging her down from the barstool and into his arms. Her dad gave the best hugs.

Although, Landon's last night had been pretty amazing too.

They were both pretty big guys, so when they engulfed her in their arms, she felt it. Before last night, she always appreciated the warmth and affection in Dad's hugs, but today, it was more than that. It made her feel safe, and it was hard for her to let go. Not that *that* was a problem. Her dad wasn't letting go either.

"If you ever walk down a dark street alone at night again, I swear to God, I'll take you over my knee and spank your ass. I don't care how old you are."

She laughed at the threat, trying to hold her tears at bay. Considering her father had never spanked her as a child—and God knew she'd tested his patience—she understood exactly how serious he was now.

"Never again," she promised, and she meant it.

"And next time," he continued, "let go of the damn purse."

"But it was a Louis Vuitton." Sunnie figured it was too soon to joke with him, but she had to try.

Dad narrowed his eyes, and she held her hands up in surrender.

"I'll let go next time."

Her response didn't help. "There'd better not *be* a next time. Not sure my heart can handle it. When your name came through dispatch as a mugging victim..." He shook his head.

"I'm okay, Dad." She gave him a quick kiss on the cheek.

"Landon take your statement yet?"

She shook her head. "No. I just got out of bed. He's waiting for me upstairs. I should probably get up there in case he has something else to do today. I got a sleepy start."

Dad gave her a kiss on the forehead, and then she gave Pop Pop another hug.

"Love you, lass," Pop Pop murmured.

As she dashed upstairs, she passed everyone else on the stairs.

"Landon's waiting for you," Finn said.

"Mom's got shepherd's pie, Sunnie," Darcy said. "Wanna have lunch with us after you talk to Landon?"

"No, I'm not hungry."

She continued on, finding Landon sitting on the edge of the couch, flipping through the TV channels. He turned it off when she walked in and started to rise. She gestured for him to stay where he was.

"So, what do we need to do for this?"

Landon picked up a notebook from the end table and asked her a series of questions. She told him everything as it had happened, step by step. She tried to describe the guy, though she really hadn't gotten a great look at him—he'd had a ball cap pulled low on his face. Landon wrote it all down, and then put the notebook aside.

Everything he did and said was typical Landon, yet Sunnie couldn't stop the butterflies in her stomach that made this feel different.

Exciting.

Then he broke the pattern.

He picked up her legs, tugged off her sandals and rested her feet on his lap, as if it were the most normal thing in the world. She was about to pull them back when he gripped one firmly, rubbing it so perfectly, she closed her eyes in absolute bliss.

Landon pushed his thumb into one arch with more pressure, and Sunnie tried to come to grips with the way it was making her feel.

Shit. She was totally getting turned on.

She needed to stop this.

Then he dug his thumb in harder, and she moaned.

She thought her response would make him stop, but it didn't.

Instead, he did it again.

She opened her eyes and found him looking at her, studying her face.

"What are you doing?"

"Foot rub."

She narrowed her eyes. It felt like more than that.

Landon's hands moved from one foot to the other, treating it to the same amazing rub, and she stopped resisting, lying back on the couch and enjoying it.

"How's your ankle?" he asked.

"Fine. Just a little bit stiff." She sighed, happy and relaxed from his foot rub. "I think Dad and Finn are still pretty ticked off at me."

He nodded. "They'll settle down soon enough. You know Finn. He's always been over-the-top when it comes to his kid sisters. It's going to take him a little while to land."

Landon was right. Sometimes it felt as if he and Finn shared a hive mind.

Landon had grown up with his single mother, who'd worked two jobs to make ends meet, which meant Landon had spent as much time with her family as he did in his own home.

"So, you and Derek are over?"

She nodded. "Oh yeah."

"What was the fight about?"

"Same old, same old."

Landon chuckled. "Jesus. Not again."

Sunnie rolled her eyes. Ever since her first official boyfriend sophomore year, right down the line to Derek, her breakups had always been some variation of the same theme. A few months of dating, maybe some hot and heavy, and then *boom*!

The guy got serious, and she started looking for the exit.

"He wanted to be exclusive. Oh, and sleep with me."

"You and Derek never slept together?"

She shook her head. "No. Finn was right. He was a douchebag."

"Then why did you keep dating him?"

Sunnie shrugged. "Because it was easy. We'd go to the movies or dancing. He didn't want a relationship and neither did I. Truth of the matter was, we didn't even talk that much. Just sort of hung out. And he wasn't hard to look at."

Landon pushed her feet off his lap and reached for her hand, pulling her until she was sitting up. "Why are you so against relationships, Sunnie?"

"I'm not against them at all. I only graduated from college last month and I want to focus on my career, want to take some time to be a nurse. Look at my family, Landon. You know as well as I do how this is going to go down."

"Go down?" he repeated, confused.

"I'm a Collins. There's a curse. We fall in love and that's it. Game over. Marriage, kids, forever. I'm not ready for that. I just want to be a nurse for now, sow a few wild oats, have a good time. I'm only twenty-five, for heaven's sake."

"Okay. I get that. Actually, that makes a lot of sense. I always thought you were anti-marriage."

She didn't realize that was the vibe she'd been sending out. "Of course I'm not. I come from a great family and my parents are an amazing couple. Why wouldn't I want that? Eventually," she added. "I'm just not super mushy-gushy about romance, like you."

He rolled his eyes, used to her teasing him. "Very funny."

"Actually, I think it's sweet that you keep trying to make every woman you date 'the one'."

"I don't do that."

"Liar, liar pants on fire."

Landon's mom had gotten pregnant in high school. The sperm donor walked away, leaving a very jaded, very down-on-relationships Ms. Riggs behind. Her stance on that hadn't changed until Landon was in high school, and his mom married a divorcee with two grown sons in college.

For some reason, Landon had gone the opposite way. As much as his mother rebuffed dating and relationships, Landon embraced them. Where Sunnie had a long list of short-term boyfriends, Landon had a short list of long-term girlfriends—three, to be exact.

Sunnie suspected he would have proposed marriage to Audrey, if she hadn't broken things off. Or maybe it was more accurate to say they'd drifted apart because they'd simply wanted different things out of life. Baltimore had never been Audrey's final destination. An aspiring actress, she'd headed to New York, desperate to make it on Broadway.

And while Landon had toyed with following her—both Sunnie and Finn terrified he would leave—Landon knew he wouldn't be happy in the Big Apple. Baltimore was home, and he was as devoted to the city as Sunnie was.

Audrey had gone anyway and broken his heart, but Sunnie knew Audrey had been devastated as well. Why wouldn't she be? Landon was a great guy.

And he gave stellar foot rubs.

And...

"Should we talk about that kiss?" Sunnie said, deciding they might as well address the elephant in the room.

He shook his head. "Nothing to say. You were being a pain in the ass and I put a stop to it. That's all there was to it."

That didn't feel like all. Ever since April Fools, it felt like something had shifted between them. "That's kind of a weird way to shut someone up."

Landon closed his eyes, and she realized he looked really tired. Chances were good he hadn't slept any better than she had.

He was a true friend. More than that, he was an honorary brother.

Or at least he had been. Until those two kisses.

"Yeah. I know." He opened his eyes, his gaze capturing hers. "I've been thinking about it. Last night, you were pissed at Derek and you took off down that dark street. It was an impulsive reaction. Can you just accept it was the same for me? I saw that guy push you down, saw that mark on your face," he reached out and touched the bruise gently, "and I reacted. I was terrified and relieved at the same time. It came out like that."

"So...no more kisses?"

He didn't reply immediately and when he did, she wasn't sure what to make of his response. "If that's what you want."

What she wanted?

Wasn't that what he wanted too?

"I don't want this to change things between us," she said. Landon wasn't like other guys to her. She would never risk their friendship on a few kisses...or more.

"Okay. And just for the record, you don't have to run out immediately and find some other gym rat like Derek to date just to hold me at bay."

"I didn't..." Sunnie didn't finish her statement, his words sparking something she hadn't considered. After April Fools, she had latched on to Derek because he'd been there...and it made it easy for her to pretend that kiss with Landon hadn't happened.

She recalled every second of the kiss, but she'd lied, pretended to *not* remember because it was the only way she could handle what it had done to her.

Landon captured her gaze. "Yeah. You did."

She appreciated his honesty, even though it annoyed her how well he understood her. It made it hard to win a fight against him.

Then she considered his reassurance that the kiss had been impulsive. His reasoning made sense...but only if it had been *her* who had initiated the kiss. She was the one who reacted first, thought later.

That wasn't Landon.

Regardless, she decided to let him off the hook.

Because she had to.

She and Landon were practically family. More than that, they were at two completely different places in their lives at the moment. She was focusing on her career. He was looking for true love.

So it was time to forget the kisses and get things back to normal.

Somehow.

❧ 6 ☙

A week later, Sunnie threw on her scrubs and headed toward the kitchen, curious about the hushed tones she heard. People were whispering. Collinses never whispered. At least not well.

She walked into the kitchen to find Yvonne, Finn, Padraig and Darcy all standing there. They stopped talking as she walked in.

Sunnie experienced a strong feeling of déjà vu. "Didn't we just do some variation of this last week?"

Finn was frowning again. He'd bounced back from her near mugging fairly quickly, so she wasn't sure what had him looking so...concerned. Or was it confused?

"What's wrong?" she asked.

"Nothing," Darcy said too brightly, too loudly.

It was obviously a lie.

"What happened?" she pressed.

Finn ran his hand over his chin but didn't speak. Sunnie established eye contact with every person in the room, but none of them appeared prepared to tell her what was going on.

"Fine," she said at last. "I'm going to work."

Finn put a hand out, grasping her wrist. "Maybe you should call in sick today."

Sunnie became alarmed. "Why would I do that?"

He shrugged. "I just think maybe you should lay low for a little while."

"Lay low? What the hell are you talking about?"

Yvonne looked around the room, raising her eyebrows. Finn sighed, and she thought he might have cursed under his breath.

There was clearly some sort of nonverbal conversation passing between everyone.

"I'm going to lose my shit in about three seconds if someone doesn't tell me what's going on," Sunnie declared.

"She's going to find out sooner rather than later, Finn." Yvonne held out her cell phone. "You and Landon have gone viral."

"Viral?" Sunnie frowned—until she saw the headline on the YouTube video.

*Hot Cop Saves Sexy Nurse.*

"What the fuck?" Sunnie pushed play, horrified to discover someone had recorded almost everything that happened last week, starting with Landon running toward her.

Whoever filmed it was too far away to pick up their voices, so they'd superimposed a romantic song over the whole thing. While nothing they said could be heard, the person recording them was in a perfect position to pick up everything else. Landon kneeling before her, checking her for injuries, hugging her, the way he helped her stand up, the kiss—oh God, *the kiss*— and then him carrying her back toward the cruiser.

That was where it ended.

And that was when she realized where the recording had come from.

The reporter.

She glanced down at the number of views...and gasped. Yvonne hadn't exaggerated about the viral part.

"Where's Landon?" She hadn't seen him since last week, not

since the foot rub and their decision to put the kisses behind them and carry on as normal.

Of course, if they'd been truly doing that, she would have seen him at least two or three times this week and they would have texted a few times every day, but that hadn't happened. He hadn't come by. She hadn't texted. It had been a very unusual radio silence.

"I talked to him this morning," Finn said. "It was supposed to be his day off, but Dad called him into work."

"Why?"

Finn rubbed his neck, his confusion giving way to a weary expression. "The captain had some questions for him."

"About that?" she asked, pointing to the phone.

Darcy nodded.

"He can't get in trouble for that!"

Finn reached out and placed a comforting hand on her arm. "I don't think he will. I mean, when the recording first went viral, no one knew who either of you were."

"*First* went viral?" she asked.

"Someone pointed it out to me last night right before closing time," Yvonne said. "It was one of our regulars, and she made some comment about it looking like you, but she wasn't really sure."

"Why didn't you wake me up?" Sunnie asked.

"You'd had a really shitty day, and I didn't want..." Yvonne let her excuses drift away. One of Sunnie's cancer patients had passed away yesterday. She'd come home after her shift, hit the couch, cried, then gone to bed early.

"I understand why," Sunnie said, letting Yvonne know it was okay.

"This morning, someone identified Landon," Finn said.

"But not me?"

"Right now, you're still anonymous. Just known as 'sexy nurse,'" Yvonne said. She added with a grin, "That nickname is going to stick, by the way."

They laughed, prompting Sunnie to roll her eyes. "You don't seriously think I'm going to complain about that, do you?"

"Even so," Darcy added, "it's pretty obvious it's you, and now that Landon's been identified, we figure it won't be long before someone outs you."

"Is Landon in trouble?" she asked, worried about him.

"The captain knows Landon's practically a bro—" Finn cut the word "brother" short.

There was nothing brotherly about the kiss she and Landon had shared.

"That kiss didn't mean anything, Finn," she insisted quickly. Landon had offered an explanation that both of them seemed willing to live with.

Except they hadn't seen each other in a week to test the theory.

"Sunnie..." Finn started.

"I'm serious. Nothing has changed."

She had been the pest of a little sister bugging him and Finn since they were kids, and now they were friends. No. More than that. He was like another brother to her. She would never jeopardize that. No matter how amazing a kisser he was.

Unfortunately, watching the kiss on the screen only reminded her how freaking hot it was. And that horniness emotion returned.

Finn frowned, and she could see he didn't believe that the kiss was nothing.

"It's not the first time the two of you have kissed lately," Yvonne pointed out, very unhelpfully.

Sunnie narrowed her eyes. "April Fools doesn't count, Vonnie. Landon and I were both drunk and we'd overdosed on the bacon buffet. Plus, I was Jasmine—I was feeling very Dance of the Seven Veils that night. You can't hold me responsible for anything I do when I'm in Disney Princess mode."

Yvonne and Darcy laughed and agreed with that argument. Finn crossed his arms, shaking his head.

"Besides," Sunnie continued, "neither one of us even remembers it!"

She tried to hold on to that lie. The tequila had wiped away any inhibitions she might have had in regards to kissing her brother's best friend.

It was all that talk about what he liked in the bedroom. Sweet merciful heaven. He'd said the words, and it had taken everything she had not to strip off her costume right then and there.

She recalled leaning toward him, and while she'd been tipsy— okay, drunk—she was ninety-two percent certain that Landon had met her halfway. And he'd definitely been the first to introduce tongues to the kiss.

No. Crap. Maybe that had been her.

But she definitely hadn't forced him to snake his hand over her bare waist to tug her closer.

"It really doesn't mean anything?" Darcy asked. "Because it looked—"

"I was upset," she wasn't, "and he was comforting me," he wasn't, "so yes, I swear it was nothing more than that." It hadn't felt like nothing. God, it had felt incredible. And she'd wanted more. A lot more.

She squeezed her eyes shut and pushed that thought away, refusing to go down that path.

Brother. He was like a brother to her.

Funny how that word no longer felt like it applied. In fact, it felt downright wrong.

"Are you sure *Landon* would agree that it's nothing?" Finn asked.

Sunnie nodded, not sure at all. "Yes. It was a mistake. We laughed it off and now it's over."

Had they laughed? She couldn't recall.

Shit. The video could probably tell her.

Finn studied her face, and she worked hard to hold his gaze, to dare him to argue with her about it.

She was on system overload, between the near mugging, the punch, the kiss, her patient dying, the video and now...Finn's face.

Was he angry about the kiss? Upset by it?

Landon was Finn's best friend. Was her big brother feeling protective of her? Hell, was he feeling protective of Landon? Ever since graduation, they'd become a gang of three—her, Finn and Landon. She liked to joke that it had taken her over a decade to wear them down, but in the end, she'd finally made them play with her.

"It didn't look like nothing," Finn muttered.

"We're friends, Finn. That's all."

"Closer than friends," Finn corrected. "Family."

That was—and wasn't—true. Landon had never made any secret of the fact he'd wished countless times he had been born into the Collins clan. And while he'd been "adopted" into her family, there was no denying things had gotten fuzzy between the two of them lately.

Was that what Finn was worried about? That she and Landon might cross a line they couldn't step back over?

"Nothing has changed for either of us. I swear."

He nodded and she wasn't sure if she saw or imagined a look of relief on his face.

"I think I should go to the police station. Try to set things straight."

"Dad's going to be here in a few minutes, Sun," Darcy said. "He really doesn't want you to go to the precinct. Right now, no one knows who you are. If you show up, people might put one and one together and—"

"I know that, but Landon—"

"Landon isn't in trouble." It was the first time Padraig had spoken. "He saved you last week. Chased away the bad guy." He crossed the room and hugged her. He'd done the same thing the night of the mugging, but she'd been too distracted by what had happened to acknowledge the warmth of it.

She squeezed him back. "I'm fine, Paddy."

"Thank God," he murmured, his cheek pressed to the side of her head. "I couldn't stand it if anything bad happened to you."

She felt guilty for causing Padraig even a second of worry. Mia's face flashed before her eyes as she closed them, desperate to fight back the tears gathering in her lashes. She'd only known Paddy's wife a short time before she'd passed away. But that one year of friendship had been enough for Mia to leave a hole in her heart no one would ever fill. She missed her every day.

"I love you," he whispered.

Before Mia, love was something they all felt for each other, but rarely expressed out loud. Since her passing, Padraig was much freer with the words.

"I love you too, Paddy."

He kissed her on the forehead. "While you wait for Uncle Aaron, you might want to pay a little visit to someone downstairs."

She grinned. "Pop Pop?"

Padraig winked. "He's a nosy old man. Go indulge him."

Sunnie sighed. "Let me call work and see if I can trade shifts with someone. This is going to be a pain in the ass, isn't it?"

"Depends on how you look at it," Padraig said. "Stuff like this is as good or bad as you want to make it."

Her older cousin always found the best way of looking at things, putting a positive spin on stuff that always helped.

"A day off is never a bad thing," she joked. "And hey, viral is pretty much synonymous with famous."

He ruffled her hair playfully. "Atta girl. Just don't let the fame go to your head." He excused himself and headed back downstairs, Darcy and Yvonne following.

Finn still leaned against the kitchen counter. She hated seeing him so worried. Walking over, she hugged him. He wrapped her up in his arms, squeezing her tight.

"You're a pain in the ass," he murmured, making her laugh.

"I know. It's what you love best about me."

He was silent for a moment, then he released her without another word, walking out of the kitchen.

Sunnie called one of her nursing colleagues, relieved when the first person she reached out to gladly agreed to switch shifts with her.

Then she headed down to the pub.

"Hey, Pop Pop."

Her grandfather brightened up when she claimed the stool next to him. "There's my lass."

"You're here early," she said.

"You know perfectly well why I'm here, sweet girl. This nosy old man wants the…" He paused, before coming up with the expression. " The 411."

Sunnie laughed loudly, drawing Padraig's attention. He'd been shooting pensive looks in their direction ever since she sat down, but now, he was smiling as well, shaking his head, though she was certain he hadn't heard what Pop Pop said.

"The 411, huh?" she teased.

"Darcy said you've got a virus."

"Gone viral," she corrected with a grin. Then she blew out a long, slow breath. "I guess it's too much to hope you haven't seen the video."

"Ah, lass, according to your sister, everyone with the Internet has seen that video. I didn't want to be left out."

She knew exactly what part of the video her romantic grandfather was interested in hearing about. "It was a heat-of-the-moment thing, Pop Pop. I'm not sure either of us thought about it. The kiss just…happened, and now it's over."

Pop Pop nodded slowly, but there was no denying he wasn't buying a word of what she was selling. "I see. Heat of the moment."

She waited for him to contradict her, but her dad walked into the pub at that moment.

Dad approached them, frowning at her sitting in her scrubs.

She raised her hand before he could speak. "I called in sick. How's Landon?"

Dad walked around the bar counter, grabbing a mug and pouring himself a cup of coffee. "He's fine."

"Is he in trouble?"

"Oh no, sweetheart. I mean...the captain wasn't thrilled to have a Baltimore police officer touted as some heartthrob hot cop all over YouTube. In addition to the reporters lining the block outside the station, we now have about fifty women trying to meet him. But Captain Ramirez is crazy about you, and when he found out you were the 'sexy nurse' Hot Cop saved, he settled down quick enough."

Sunnie pursed her lips, trying not to laugh as her dad referred to them with the video's descriptors. Now that she knew Landon wasn't in trouble, she could relax. "He's never going to live this down, is he?"

Dad grinned. "Probably not. The recording was uploaded by the reporter doing the ride-along."

"Yeah. I figured as much."

"So at least the captain had *that* guy to rake over the coals. The reporter got his ass handed to him this morning."

"Good. Is Landon still at work?"

Dad shook his head. "No. I sent him home, suggested he lay low for the rest of the day. These viral things have to run their course. Hopefully, it will have blown over by tomorrow. So far, no one seems to have figured out who you are...outside of here and the precinct, anyway. The captain has threatened to fire anyone who leaks your name to the press."

Sunnie laughed. "I bet he did."

She got a sense her dad was waiting for her to mention the video, to offer some insight into the kiss, but she didn't know what to say.

Mom came out of the kitchen. "There's my star," she said, giving Sunnie a kiss on the cheek.

"Very funny, Mom."

"Hey, I can think of worse things than being called a sexy nurse."

Dad shook his head. "Riley. This isn't exactly a great thing. You should have seen the crowd outside the station. If they find out Sunnie's the nurse, God only knows what kind of mess you'll have outside the pub."

"We've dealt with the press plenty of times before, Aaron," Pop Pop said, reassuring Dad they'd be fine and it would all blow over soon enough.

Dad took his coffee back to the kitchen, walking with Mom, who needed to continue preparing the day's specials.

Sunnie hung out with Pop Pop, joining him for a late breakfast. Padraig found an *Ellen* repeat for them on the TV, so they sat in silence watching it as they ate.

She'd just finished her meal when her phone pinged.

It was a text from Landon. The first in a week.

*You okay, sexy nurse?*

She giggled, flashing the screen to Pop Pop, who chuckled.

*Yeah. How are you holding up, hot cop?*

*Scored a day off.*

*I heard*, she texted back. *Perks of fame.*

He sent back the eye-rolling emoji, and she laughed again. Then another text came through.

*Would like to talk to you soon*

*Ok*

*Text you later*

*K*

Sunnie placed her phone on the counter and looked at the TV, not hearing or seeing anything.

"What does your young man say, lass?"

She glanced over at her grandfather. "This is Landon we're talking about, Pop Pop. He's not *my* young man. God, he's practically my brother."

Pop Pop studied her, his gaze almost piercing, but he didn't correct her. Instead, he gave an unconvinced, "Mmm-hmm."

"What?" she pressed.

"Watch the video again, Sunnie."

She frowned and picked up her phone.

He placed his hand over hers. "Not now. When you're alone and not worried about schooling your face for my benefit or anyone else's. Watch the video when there's no one around."

"I already saw it."

Pop Pop grinned. "And like ninety-nine-point-nine percent of humanity would do, I'll wager you were looking at yourself. Watch it again. And look at Landon's face."

She tried to recall what she'd seen of him the first time she'd watched the video...and realized Pop Pop was right. She'd been looking at herself. Apart from the kiss and the body language of the two of them, she hadn't really looked at Landon.

What the hell had Pop Pop seen?

And did she really want to know?

$\bf{?}$    7    $\bf{?}$

"**M**ail call, Romeo."

Landon sighed, but didn't look up from the report he was filling in on his laptop. At least, not until his partner—and so-called friend—Miguel upended a sack of mail bigger than Santa's on his desk, the surface overflowing with letters.

"What the fuck?"

"Fan mail," Miguel said with a grin that told him his partner was getting too much pleasure from this.

Landon picked up a letter, peering at the feminine handwriting. "Jesus," he muttered. He'd had to shut down his work email four days earlier when the mailbox filled up within sixteen hours. It was wreaking havoc on his ability to do his job effectively.

Apparently, the lonely hearts weren't deterred by his lack of email and had decided to go old school. Legit love letters.

It had been a week since the video of him kissing Sunnie and carrying her toward the police car had gone viral. And instead of the hubbub dying down, it had only grown worse. Sunnie's name had been leaked by a patient at Johns Hopkins, who'd recognized her as his nurse. So now, not only was there a crowd gathered daily outside the police station, but around Pat's Pub as well.

Funny enough, the pub was faring better than the police station. Of course, the Collins family had been dealing with fan mobs for decades. After all, Sky Mitchell, singer of The Universe —a band whose record sales put them on par with The Beatles, the Eagles, and the Stones—was married to Sunnie's aunt. Then they'd had those tabloid-chaser skills tested again last year when Teagan's daughter, Ailis, started dating Hunter Maxwell, a huge up-and-comer on the music scene.

The problem with Sunnie's name becoming public meant the scrutiny on both of them was now intense. He didn't dare go to the pub because of all the eyes watching. The last thing they needed was a bunch of yahoos fighting to get close enough to snag a photo or bombard them with personal questions.

He wanted to protect her privacy as much as he could, but he hated that he hadn't seen her since the morning after the attack. He'd stayed away after the mugging thinking a break might bring him some clarity about the kisses...and about his newfound feelings for her.

Two weeks. He hadn't seen her in two weeks and all he'd done was think about her nonstop.

Sunnie had been like a sister to him for most of his life, but ever since that drunken kiss at April Fools, the blinders had fallen off. Now he wanted to do a fairly long list of dirty, dirty things with her that would have both Finn and Aaron kicking his ass.

The time away hadn't helped. Not even a little bit.

"What the hell am I supposed to do with all this?" Landon asked.

Miguel started opening some of the letters, reading them aloud to the other cops.

Mandy, the dispatcher, walked by laughing. "It's just like *Sleepless in Seattle.*"

Sadly, Landon knew that movie all too well. It was his mother's favorite.

"Hey, Landon," Miguel said. "If you're not going to call," his partner glanced at the signature of the letter he was reading, "Ashley, you mind if I do?"

Landon stood up and ripped the letter out of Miguel's hand. "This isn't a joke, man."

"If you can't laugh at *this*," Miguel said, pointing to the mountain of letters, "you're going to be in trouble."

"This was supposed to blow over in a day or two."

"That was the captain's estimate. And Aaron's. I could have told you fifteen minutes of fame in this climate can last a few weeks, maybe months. You and Sunnie are serious YouTube superstars. When those top-of-the-charts shows start counting down the most viral videos in history, you two are going to rank right up there with 'Charlie Bit Me' and 'Evolution of Dance'."

"Shit." Landon had hit his limit. Between the women following him everywhere, proposing everything from marriage to kinky sex acts he'd had to look up on Urban Dictionary, and the requests for interviews and photo shoots, he was running on very little sleep and less patience.

Miguel kept sifting through the letters. His eyes lit up. "Ooh la la. One from a dude. You *gotta* give me this one. You're straight."

Miguel liked to brag that he straddled every line. Half-black, half-Hispanic. Bisexual. The guy said he could tick every minority box out there, and he loved it.

"Take the letter. Take them all. This is getting on my nerves."

"Look on the bright side," Miguel said, leaning on the edge of his desk. "Everyone has forgotten about the bumper sticker."

Landon scowled. "You know what? Let's go back to that. I prefer the bumper sticker jokes."

Miguel's eyes widened. "Damn man. Never thought I'd hear you ask for that."

He and Finn had had a practical joke war running since junior year of high school, and currently, Finn was one up.

The son of a bitch had slapped a bumper sticker on his car of a weed plant with the words "Fuck the Cops." Landon hadn't noticed it, but the state police had, and they'd pulled him over for going five measly miles over the speed limit. When they'd run his license and discovered he was a cop too, they'd pointed out the bumper sticker, amused to find out it was a prank.

They'd managed to tell enough fellow officers that the story got back to this precinct. For the past few months, Landon had been barraged with marijuana brochures, flyers, and other weed-themed knickknacks from the other cops, who had shown no signs of letting the joke die. Until now.

Cops were like dogs with a bone when they got ahold of shit like this.

The fucking reporter had added background music to the video of him with Sunnie. If he never heard Faith Hill's "This Kiss" again, it would be too soon.

Some wiseass—he suspected Miguel—kept changing Landon's ringtone to the song, and someone had decorated the men's stalls in the bathroom with memes created from screenshots from the video and lyrics from the song. No matter how many times he tore them down, they kept going up.

Or at least they had—until Aaron found them and put a stop to it once and for all.

"Did I convince you to do that calendar thing yet?" Miguel asked.

Landon shook his head. A photographer who was putting together a sexy blue-collar calendar had approached him. She'd rounded up beefcake firefighters, construction workers, fishermen, and coal miners from all over the country. She had asked him to represent the cops. "They want me to pose shirtless, Miguel, with my gun belt unhooked. I'd feel like a jackass."

"Yeah, but...she's giving you December. Bet you could convince her to let you lie on a bearskin rug in front of a fire."

"You're hilarious. It's not happening. I'll do the basketball game."

Miguel was unimpressed. "You do that every year, asshole."

Each year, the firefighters and the cops played a charity game to raise money for cancer research. Sunnie was an oncology nurse, and she'd shared stories about the patients on her floor, what they went through, how brave they were. It was a cause he could definitely get behind.

"Just ask the calendar photographer to give your portion of the proceeds to a charity of your choice. Start using your fame for good."

Miguel should have been the one to go viral. He had the right personality for it. Hell, so did Sunnie. Finn said she was getting a kick out of her time in the spotlight, posing for pictures and even going so far as to sing "This Kiss" at the pub's monthly karaoke night. Landon had been relieved—and sorry—he'd missed it.

"I'll think about it," he said at last, just to get Miguel off his back about it for a little while longer.

Mandy looked up from her desk, her hand over the microphone part of her headset. "Landon, I swear to God, I've got someone from *Ellen* on the phone asking if you and Sunnie would want to make an appearance."

Landon leaned back in his chair, defeated, rubbing his eyes with one hand. "Fuck."

"Landon?" Mandy called out. "What should I say?"

"Tell them no!" he yelled back, his heated response enough to reduce the noisy room to silence.

Feeling bad for his tone, he added, "Please, Mandy," but it was too late.

"Riggs. My office."

Landon looked up at Miguel. "Aaron was behind me listening to all that, wasn't he?"

Miguel nodded, not bothering to wipe away his grin.

"For how long?"

"Let's just say I think you might be doing that calendar."

"You're a prick, Miguel."

"I love you too, man."

Landon laughed, despite his annoyance. Truth was, he and

Miguel had become pretty good friends in the past year since Miguel had joined the force and they'd been partnered up.

Landon walked into Aaron's office. "I'm sorry about—"

"Shut the door, Landon."

He turned and did as commanded, then took the chair Aaron gestured to. The two of them faced each other across Aaron's large desk, the surface piled high with file folders and paper.

"This isn't dying down."

If it had been anyone other than Aaron speaking, Landon's natural response would have been "no shit, Sherlock." However, he'd never speak so disrespectfully to his boss and mentor.

"No," he said, "it's not."

"We're going to have to find a way to draw the line of fire away from here. This is a police station, Landon. Not the set of *Big Brother*."

Landon grimaced. "I realize that."

"I think it would be best if you took some time off until this whole thing blows over. I can't have the dispatch line tied up with reporters, single women, the tabloids and Ellen's people, trying to get ahold of you."

Landon panicked. This job was his life. "Are you suspending me?" he asked in alarm.

"No. Of course not. But I looked at your file and you have a couple weeks of vacation time coming to you. Take a week of it. If *you* stop showing up here, maybe those reporters and women outside will get bored and start staying home too."

Landon sighed. If he stopped showing up here, they'd just surround his apartment.

He wanted his normal life back.

"Aaron, listen, I don't think—" he started.

"This isn't up for debate, Landon. Shit's getting out of hand here. Started with everyone wanting to know who hot cop was, then Sunnie's name was leaked, now her relationship to me and the fact I'm your boss. I'm not telling either one of you to talk to the media, but your silence seems to be sparking a firestorm in terms of speculation and fairy tales. You know what I read this morning? Fucking Yahoo news is running some click-bait article about me being outraged by your 'secret relationship' with my daughter. I've been cast as the villain, working against some illicit love affair. Fuckers even found an old driver's license photo of me. The bad one that Riley has teased me about for years, claiming I look like a seventies porn star."

Landon couldn't help it. He laughed. He'd seen that picture, and Riley hadn't lied. "I'm still not sure why you thought a mustache was a good idea."

"I've told all of you a million times. I lost a goddamn bet to Tris. Had to sport that fucking thing for six months. I can't help it that's when my license renewal came up!"

"I'm sorry about the article." Landon hated to think about Aaron being portrayed as an asshole. Aaron was the most upright, honest man he knew. Landon spent his entire childhood wishing Aaron was his father. Even when his mother remarried, it was still Aaron he had turned to whenever he had a "guy" question he couldn't ask his mom. Aaron had taught him and Finn how to drive, how to shave. He'd snuck them boxes of condoms when he'd found out they'd both started fooling around with girls. While his mother had—awkwardly—given him the sex talk, it was Aaron who'd answered the twelve thousand questions he'd had afterwards.

Aaron sighed and stood up, walking to the window. "I think you need to change your attitude about all of this."

"What do you mean?"

"Miguel had a point out there. It's time to start laughing about the whole thing. I can see you're working your ass off, trying to do your job. I appreciate that. But the cards are stacked against you right now. So embrace it. Enjoy it. You haven't been by the pub all week. Why not?"

"I didn't think it was a good idea for me and Sunnie to be in the same place while those tabloid guys are hanging around. Thought I should try to protect her privacy."

Aaron snorted. "Have you ever known my girl to shy away from a crowd? She was down in the pub last night signing autographs."

Landon chuckled. Of course Sunnie would embrace the situation, rather than run. But the women chasing him had been tenacious.

Then he had a disquieting thought.

If *he* was being inundated by female attention, was she getting hit on by countless guys?

"It's the women more than the photographers," Landon admitted. "I swear to God, I found two of them going through my garbage outside this morning. And I had to kill my Instagram because some of the pics I was getting tagged on were..."

Aaron gave him a sympathetic nod. "Yeah. I get what you're saying. The tabloids are one thing. The women...well, I'm afraid I'm not sure how to help single hot cop in regards to all that."

Landon sighed—then stilled, replaying the comment.

*Single hot cop.*

*Single.*

"You are still single, aren't you?" Aaron asked.

And there it was. Landon had waited a week for this particular shoe to drop. Aaron hadn't mentioned the kiss until this moment.

"I, um...well...uh..."

Wow. He'd had a whole week to come up with an answer and that was all he could manage.

Aaron walked over and placed a hand on his shoulder. "Yeah. That's what I thought. Go to the pub, Landon. Kick back a few pints with Finn and Sunnie. Hiding from women is one thing, but hiding from your friends is another. Let Sunnie show you how it's done. I figure the two of you are tied together by what's happened. You need to be around someone who gets what you're going through, and right now, that's her."

Was Aaron talking about the video or confusion over the kiss?

Then he saw the truth of Aaron's observation. He'd spent a week feeling like a bug under a microscope. He was miserable with the constant scrutiny. Sunnie had obviously found a way to make it fun.

Like she did everything.

Suddenly he understood why his mood had been getting progressively blacker with each passing day. He missed Sunnie.

And that's when the answer came to him.

Sunnie had a fun-loving, larger-than-life personality. He needed her silly perspective on all of this to get him through. But more than that...he needed to erase the word *single* from hot cop.

Maybe forever.

The problem was Sunnie wouldn't come around easily. So he'd have to trick her into it.

And he had the perfect plan.

Sunnie was about to pay him back for saving her from the mugger by going out with him. Having Sunnie pose as his girlfriend would hopefully get the hot-cop groupies off his back. But more than that, it would show Sunnie something that the two of them should have recognized all along.

They belonged together.

Life was about to get a lot more fun.

❧ 8 ❧

Sunnie sat in a booth at Pat's Pub with a couple of her nursing friends, enjoying a Friday night happy hour, complete with big-ass margaritas. Her weekend off had just gotten extended to a week, thanks to that damn video. She intended to kick it off in style.

She glanced around the pub, looking for Landon. It had become a bad habit of hers, ever since the mugging and that kiss. Probably because he hadn't darkened her door once in the past two weeks. The guy was a regular fixture in her life, stopping by the Collins Dorm every couple of nights. This was the longest he'd stayed away.

And it was fucking with her head.

Giving her too much time to think.

Sunnie was *pretty* sure when she *did* see him, everything between them would be cool. Same as always.

Maybe.

Shit. Hopefully.

It was the damn kisses she was fixated on. Sunnie hadn't watched the video since seeing it on Yvonne's phone in the kitchen. She'd pulled out her laptop at least a hundred times, intent on doing what Pop Pop suggested.

*Watch it again.*

*Look at Landon's face.*

She couldn't make herself do it, too afraid of what she'd see.

"Sunshine?"

Wow. It was as if she'd thought his name and summoned him. Somehow he'd come into the bar and walked right up to her table without her noticing.

"Hey, Landon," Yvonne said, hip bumping him as she passed with a tray of appetizers for the table next to them. "Long time, no see."

Landon grinned and said hello, chatting for just a minute with her cousin and her friends at the table.

Sunnie took advantage of the time to check him out. He looked great, wearing dark jeans and a collared short-sleeved shirt that accentuated his muscular arms. Somewhere along the line, he'd stopped shaving.

"You have a beard," Sunnie said, interrupting him as he and Yvonne chatted about last night's baseball game.

*Way to state the obvious.*

He stopped talking, and Yvonne gave her a curious look as she continued on with her tray. Landon rubbed his jaw, nodding. "Haven't shaved since that damn video went viral. Thought it might help disguise me."

"Is it working?"

Landon chuckled. "I'm not sure. Should we ask the fifteen women who followed me to the pub just now?"

She and her friends laughed.

Landon looked great, handsome and in good spirits. It appeared he was taking the fallout from the video in stride, handling the constant scrutiny better than she thought he was. Finn had led her to believe Landon wasn't happy with all the photographers and women crowding the sidewalks outside his apartment and work.

Not that she was surprised. Landon had always been the

quieter of the three of them, calmer, more introspective. Finn joked it was because he lacked the tainted Collins blood.

"Do you mind if I steal Sunnie for a minute?" Landon asked her girlfriends.

They both shook their heads, giving her looks that said they would definitely be demanding details upon her return. She'd already spent the better part of this week assuring her family, friends and work colleagues that the kiss had meant nothing.

It was funny that repeating that same thing over and over hadn't convinced her it was the truth. In fact, it made her question what the kisses meant even more.

She stood up, allowing him to pull her to a table in a quiet corner of the pub.

"No work today?"

He shook his head. "Your dad made me take a vacation. Think he's sick of the constant crowd of tabloid photographers on the sidewalk outside the precinct."

Sunnie took a sip of the margarita she'd carried over with her when Yvonne approached and asked Landon he if wanted anything. He ordered a pint of Guinness and Yvonne went to get it.

Sunnie put down her nearly full glass. "I got the same invitation to stay away from the hospital today. My nursing supervisor said if she wanted to deal with that much paparazzi, she would have hired a Kardashian. She was joking, but even so, she was glad when the hospital granted me a week's leave."

"Fate is smiling on us. That's how much time I've got off too."

She gave him a funny look. "What's fate got to do with it?"

He leaned forward, resting his elbows on the table. "We're going to beat this thing. Together."

"Beat it?"

"Yep. You owe me."

Sunnie was confused. "Excuse me?"

"I wouldn't be in this mess if you hadn't decided to take a

walk on the wild side the other night and fought that guy for your purse."

She matched his position, leaning toward him. "Oh no. None of this is *my* fault, Romeo. If you hadn't laid that damn kiss on me in front of that reporter, that video wouldn't have gone viral and we wouldn't be in this situation. So really, it's you who owes *me*."

He shook his head, refusing to listen to her reasoning. "You kissed me at the April Fools party. We're calling the kisses a draw."

She narrowed her eyes. "I thought you didn't remember the kiss at the party."

Landon shrugged. "I lied."

That response took her aback for a second. "I didn't initiate that kiss."

"Yes, you did."

Sunnie tried to figure out how to feel about the fact he'd remembered the kiss. She really thought she'd dodged a bullet there. To find out that she hadn't—and now he'd added his own kiss to the hot mess they were making of this friendship—was surprising...and interesting.

Landon was Mr. Rock Solid, meaning he was so reliable, so true to character, she could set a watch by him. She could pretty much predict how he was going to react to any and every situation.

Except this one.

She would have thought he'd hunker down and hide out while giving the whole viral thing a chance to blow over. That didn't appear to be his plan. More than that, he was trying to game the system. That was a Sunnie move, not a Landon one.

"You've gone quiet. Not sure I've ever heard that lack of sound from you." He laughed at his own joke, and her body responded to it in a very uncomfortable, hot-and-bothered way. Dammit. She'd really thought these past two weeks would help her get over all these...unwanted feelings.

She decided to hear him out, curious about where he was going with this whole "you owe me" thing. "What do you want?"

"You're going to pretend to be my girlfriend until all this shit blows over and the lovestruck mob following me goes away."

She shook her head. "Nope."

"Yes. You are. This 'single hot cop' thing isn't getting better. It's getting worse. The best way to tackle it is to go on the offensive. If I'm not single, if I'm, in fact, dating sexy nurse, those women hovering outside my apartment will realize I'm not available and hopefully back off."

"And what if they don't?" she asked.

"I'm not worried about that. You're going to be a very jealous girlfriend."

Sunnie rolled her eyes, waiting for the "I'm just kidding" that would prove this was all some big gag at her expense. "Did Finn put you up to this?"

Landon shook his head. "No. It was actually something your dad said at work. He was the one who pointed out the appeal of a single hot cop."

"And he suggested we pretend to date?" Sunnie felt as if she should step outside to see if a meteor was streaking across the sky, headed for their planet. Landon had studied his predictable-as-the-tide skills under her father's tutelage, the perfect Padawan to Dad's Jedi master.

"Of course not. He just got me thinking that the best way to combat the problem is to take the word *single* away."

"So go find a girlfriend."

He tilted his head, raising his eyebrows. "I just did. You."

Sunnie leaned back. "It'll never work. None of our family and friends will believe it for a second."

"I'm not trying to convince them. Just the strangers."

"So what are you thinking...exactly? Spell it out for me. Give me the parameters."

"Go out with me tonight. Dinner date."

"And?" she prompted.

"We'll hash out the details there."

Sunnie laughed. "So basically you have no plan."

Landon shook his head. "I have a plan, but I'm hungry and there's no reason we shouldn't get this show on the road now. The sooner the better."

She glanced over at the table she'd just left. Her girlfriends had struck up a conversation with a couple of guys at the table next to them. Neither of them would miss her. Hell, at this point, she'd be a third wheel.

"Fine." She pointed to her scrubs. "I need a minute to change."

"Cool. I'll wait down here, finish my beer."

Sunnie stood up slowly, still expecting him to spring the joke, to let her off the hook. When he simply gave her a pleasant smile, it started to sink in he really thought this was a good idea. "Okay."

She started to turn, to head toward the stairs at the back of the pub that would lead up to her apartment, but he grasped her wrist.

"Aren't you forgetting something?" he asked.

Sunnie looked longingly at the unfinished margarita. He'd said he was hungry, so she thought that was her cue to hurry up. "Yeah, I guess—"

"Not the drink." Landon pointed to his cheek. "My goodbye kiss."

She narrowed her eyes. "You can't possibly be serious."

"If we're doing this, Sunnie, we're doing it right, making it look real."

"Who the fuck are you and where did you put Landon?"

He chuckled, but didn't relent. It was clear the man actually intended for her to kiss him. She sighed. "Fine. Whatever." She leaned toward him and gave him a quick kiss on the cheek, trying to ignore how good he smelled.

Was he wearing cologne? Did he always wear it?

The second she finished, he turned his face, his lips grazing hers in a super-fast but surprisingly sweet—and hot—kiss.

She reared back. "Kissing is part of your plan?"

He looked at her like she was insane. "Of course it is. By the way, we're walking to the restaurant tonight, and you're holding my hand."

Sunnie realized that pretty much everything Landon had said to her since they'd sat down had been phrased not as a question, but as a statement.

If she didn't know him so well, she'd think he was one of those alpha male types, but this was Landon. He was the king of manners and politeness, constantly asking others what they wanted to do and phrasing most things with "please" and "thank you."

None of that was present right now.

Then she recalled his description of how he liked things in the bedroom. She'd had some very happy times with her vibrator the past couple of months, fantasizing about that list...while trying to forget Landon was the dream guy doing them to her.

She belatedly crinkled her nose, pretending to think the idea of holding his hand was gross, but his smug smile never wavered.

"I'll be right here when you come back down."

She wished that reassurance didn't set butterflies fluttering in her stomach. She felt like a teenager going on her first date.

Ugh.

Landon.

It was freaking Landon.

She didn't bother to say anything else. Instead, she flipped a casual wave and walked away, deciding this plan of his wasn't a good one.

So...she needed to form a plan of her own.

She grinned, considering the parameters they planned to set tonight over dinner. She knew exactly how to bring Landon back to his senses. She'd make a few demands of her own.

She had to.

Because Sunnie had become as obsessed with the viral kiss as those lonely hearts following him around. However, unlike those women, she had something to lose. Something pretty major.

Landon.

LANDON HADN'T BEEN ALONE AT THE TABLE MORE THAN thirty seconds when Finn plopped down in the seat Sunnie had just vacated.

"What gives?"

He'd seen Finn walk into the pub just a few minutes earlier. Finn had stopped by the bar for the pint of Guinness in his hand. And he'd seen the kiss he and Sunnie had just shared.

Another kiss. This was becoming a habit.

"What do you mean?" Landon decided to play dumb, drive Finn crazy. He figured he had at least fifteen minutes to kill before Sunnie came back down. He might as well have some fun.

"You just kissed my sister. Again."

"I know."

Finn leaned back in the chair and rubbed his jaw, his expression the textbook definition of confused. "Are you two dating?"

Landon chuckled and shook his head. "Not exactly."

He probably should have chosen his words more carefully, because Finn misinterpreted them, his eyes narrowing angrily. "You better not be fucking—"

Landon put his hands up, a sign of surrender. "Come on, man. You know me better than that," he said quickly. "Sunnie is going to help me scare away the damn groupies."

"How?"

"She and I are going to pretend we're dating."

Finn took a sip of his beer as he chewed over that piece of information. "I don't think that's a good idea."

"It's a great idea," Landon insisted. "The tabloids keep trying to put us together in some forbidden love affair, so we're just going to give it to them. Hopefully, this will scare off the women chasing me. What's more boring than a couple going out to dinner and to the movies? With any luck, this will help things blow over quicker."

"They're going to blow over on their own anyway. I can't see any reason to push the issue."

"It's driving me crazy, Finn. I'm not like you and Sunnie. I can't stand being in the spotlight."

"You just have to give it time. This shit never goes on for that long. People have very short attention spans."

Landon shrugged. "I know. And I'm going to try to make them even shorter."

Finn ran his finger through the condensation on his mug, quiet for a few moments, before looking at him again. "Are you sure that's why you're doing this?"

Landon frowned. "What's that mean? What other reason would there be?"

"You keep kissing her, man."

Glancing across the pub, Landon tried to figure out how to explain it to Finn. God, he'd like to find a way to explain it to himself. He'd kissed her at that damn party and...God...he just woke up.

But he wasn't going to say any of that to Finn. He hadn't even told Sunnie that his feelings for her had changed. So, he'd deflect. For now. "We were drunk the first time. We don't even—"

Finn held up his hand, looking slightly annoyed. "Don't bother trying to feed me that line of shit about not remembering. I know you, bro. Maybe better than you know yourself. You remember every second of that kiss. And so does Sunnie. We let you get away with denying it because you were both drunk, and it was an easy way to let you off the hook on something neither one of you should have done to begin with."

Landon tried to figure out why Finn's comment bugged him so much. Did he really believe they shouldn't have kissed? Why?

Landon knew they were a mismatch in terms of romance.

Knew they both wanted different things right now. Knew that the relationship they shared now was special and not something to fuck with. He knew all of that.

But that knowledge vanished whenever he looked at her.

"I get it," Landon said at last, simply because it was what Finn wanted to hear. And because Finn was his best friend, he knew it was a lie.

Finn shook his head. "No. You don't. Sunnie is a chronic dater, Landon. Her track record on commitment sucks."

Landon didn't think it was a commitment issue as much as bad taste on her part. "She picks gym rats, guys who can't walk by a mirror without flexing. Personally, I didn't mind that she wouldn't commit to the lumberjack, Stunt Man and Naked Ned. They were all clueless assholes."

Finn snorted as Landon listed Sunnie's last few boyfriends, using the nicknames he and Finn had given them.

"You're missing the point. The reason she goes for that type is because there's no danger of feeling anything for them. She's my sister, and I know for a fact she's never fallen in love. Not once."

Landon thought back and realized Finn was right. He hadn't considered that obstacle. Until recently, Sunnie's love life had been a source of entertainment more than something he'd seriously thought about. "That doesn't mean she won't fall in love...someday."

Finn took a swig of beer, and Landon got the sense he was using the drink as a way of stalling until he could figure out how to say what he was thinking. "I really want her to find the perfect guy to fall in love and settle down with."

Landon looked away, his feelings hurt that Finn didn't consider him fit for that role.

Until Finn continued, "And I want the same thing for you. I thought Audrey was perfect for you, and I'm sorry she chose her career over you, sorry that things between the two of you didn't work out."

Landon nodded. "She wanted to be in New York and I wanted to be here." It was strange to realize it had only taken that one thing to drive them apart. They'd been compatible right down the line, and Landon had spent the three years they'd dated certain that she was the woman he was going to marry, to have babies with. She'd been his first true love, and his first serious heartbreak.

"You haven't dated anyone since her."

"What are you getting at, Finn?"

"Honest to God, Landon, if I thought it would work, there's no one on earth I'd want to date my sister more than *you*. You're honest, faithful, a good guy. But you're looking for..."

"Forever," Landon finished.

"And Sunnie's just looking for a good time," Finn added. "At least for now. I'm not sure Sunnie would respond well to your all-in approach to relationships. The second a romance turns too serious, she finds a million reasons to run."

"I'm aware of that." He'd had a ringside seat to every single one of Sunnie's relationships. He'd heard her opinions on dating, love and sex countless times. She was a free spirit, devoted to her career, and she was showing no signs of being ready to settle down.

And even if she did, it would probably be with someone more like her, someone who loved to go dancing and party until dawn. While Landon didn't mind that on occasion, his favorite nights were the ones he spent at home on his couch, beer in hand, football game on the television. Sunnie would spontaneously combust in that lifestyle. None of that knowledge was helping him.

"I love my sister, Landon. I'm crazy about the insane girl, but that doesn't mean I'm blind to..." He sighed. "I'm not sure what to call them. They aren't faults, they're just who she is."

"I'm crazy about her too," Landon admitted. "And I get where you're coming from." Landon hated everything about this conversation. Finn was speaking logically, offering very valid points.

Unfortunately, none of it was sinking in.

When Finn kept looking at him with worried eyes, Landon gave his best friend what he needed. Reassurance. "I'm not going to throw away a lifetime friendship, Finn. I swear."

Landon understood there was too much to lose if things went south. It wouldn't just mess things up between him and Sunnie; it would be a strain on his friendship with Finn. And God, he didn't want to think about how Aaron's feelings might change toward him.

Finn nodded, clearly not reassured. "You're still going forward with this silly plan, aren't you?"

Landon nodded. He could make a long list of why it was smarter to step away. He could pit the countless items on that list against the one reason he had for moving forward. And the latter would wipe away all the rest.

He wouldn't stay away from Sunnie because he couldn't.

He was in love with her.

Sunnie held Landon's hand all the way to the restaurant, and even smiled at him fondly as he wrapped his arm around her waist when they crossed a street. They'd been followed by a handful of tabloid photographers.

She suspected most people suddenly cast into the limelight from viral videos weren't placed under this kind of scrutiny, but once it came out that she was Sky Mitchell and Teagan Collins's niece, it elevated her to some sort of reality TV status. Countless times in the past week, she'd been stopped by people wanting to know everything from what Sky and Teagan thought of her secret romance, to if she'd manufactured the video in some crazy attempt to become as famous as her relatives.

People were insane. And they fixated on weird-ass shit.

So between her famous aunt and uncle and the fact Hot Cop worked for her dad, they'd inadvertently found too many ways to keep the tabloids interested. She also figured it would only take one uncovered affair or spectacular divorce in Hollywood to move the spotlight away from them.

They stepped into Charleston, a very posh upscale restaurant in Baltimore, and she blew out a soft whistle. "Very elegant," she whispered. "And expensive. Are you sure you wouldn't rather hit The Cheesecake Factory?"

He rolled his eyes, and then turned to ask the host for a table. The host clearly recognized them and decided to buy some free publicity for the restaurant by placing them at a cozy little table near the front, right next to the windows. It gave them a great view of the waterfront—and everyone outside a perfect way to watch Sunnie and Landon.

Landon actually seemed pleased with the placement, which made sense, given his desire to speed along the news they were dating. She spotted dark circles under his eyes and realized this had probably been harder on him than he was letting on.

Once they were seated, he reached across the table and took her hand in his, a very romantic gesture that she didn't doubt every photographer outside had managed to snap a shot of.

"Smooth move," she murmured, prompting him to laugh.

Landon had a great laugh, and it did wonders at breaking the tension she'd been feeling up until that moment. She was being silly, letting the past couple of weeks blind her to something that should have been obvious. Landon was one of her best friends and this crazy-ass situation wasn't going to change that.

He ordered a bottle of wine from the waiter. When the man walked away, she leaned forward. "Wine? Seriously? I'm pretty sure they serve Guinness here."

"It's a date, Sunnie. We're going to do it right."

They chatted about the weather and work briefly, then the waiter returned with the wine, pouring it. They asked for a few more minutes with the menu and the man went away.

Sunnie decided it was time to get the show on the road. "I believe we were going to lay out the parameters of this thing."

"I was."

He'd purposely changed her pronoun. So adorable, she thought. Poor boy probably thought she'd let him get away with that. He really should know better.

"So what's our time limit?" she pressed.

"We pretend to date until this," he jerked his head to the small crowd that had formed across the street, "goes away."

"That's too nebulous. I think we need an actual time frame. One week? Two?"

Landon shook his head. "No. No set time limit. When the crowd goes away, we go back to normal."

She leaned back, debating whether or not to play her big card this early in the game. Then she decided what the hell. This could save a lot of time in the long run—because there was no way Landon was going to accept her conditions for this fake relationship.

"That could take some time," she mused.

He shrugged as if that didn't matter.

"I mean, if I'm pretending to date you, that means I can't date anyone else."

Landon frowned. "You and Derek broke up. Neither one of us is currently seeing anyone. I'm not sure why that's a problem."

"I'm just going to go ahead and lay it all on the line for you, babe." She did a little gesture toward her lap. "I'm going to need orgasms."

Landon had picked up his wineglass, intent on taking a sip, but he put it back down. "Play with your vibrators."

She shook her head. "Those are okay for a night or two, but you know me, Landon. I suck at diets. All diets. Sure, I can exist on lettuce for a day or two, but after a few days, I'm going to cave and order the large fries at McDonalds."

"Sunshine, I'm not having sex with you. That crosses way over the line of pretending."

She picked up her wineglass, running a finger over the rim. "I didn't say anything about sex. Just orgasms."

"That still crosses a line."

Sunnie lifted one shoulder. "I don't think so. It's just one friend helping out another. After all, you're the one insisting on playing this game rather than letting things run their natural course. I shouldn't have to suffer simply by going along with it."

"I hardly think using a vibrator for a week or two is suffering."

She smiled, smelling success. Landon would refuse, she'd convince him pretending to be a couple was a bad idea, they'd have a nice dinner, and she'd find some way to get her head screwed on straight about Landon again.

"We'll never agree on that, so I guess that settles it," she said. "We ca—"

"Fine. Orgasms."

Two words had never hit her with the force of those. Was he seriously giving in to her insane demand?

He studied her face, way too closely.

Dammit. The fucker was calling her bluff.

She wasn't going to lose this battle. "Wonderful. We'll start tonight after dinner. We can go back to my apartment." There was no way in hell he'd walk into the Collins Dorm and straight back to her bedroom. For one thing, they'd never get the door closed. Finn would drag both of them out and read them the riot act for being so stupid.

Besides, she wasn't sure *she* would let it go that far.

There was a big difference between these stolen kisses of his and, well, *that*.

He wasn't wrong. Orgasms *totally* crossed a line. That's why she'd suggested them to begin with. Steady, predictable Landon would never go that far.

"No," Landon said. "Not tonight. You haven't even started," he finger quoted the next two words, "'to diet.' Give the vibrator a workout and we'll revisit this later."

"I've been on the diet ever since the mugging…actually, no. It was way before that. I told you Derek and I never indulged."

"Your shitty taste in guys isn't my problem."

Sunnie grinned. "It is now." She pointed one finger downwards. "She's very hungry."

Landon laughed. "Do you really think this is going to scare me away?"

She scowled. "Yeah, babe. I'm pretty sure it will. Admit it, you're sweating bullets right now, thinking about carrying through on my demand. This whole idea is silly, Landon. It's never going to work. For one thing, we—"

"Go to the bathroom."

He kept interrupting her. With unexpected comments.

"What?"

"Get up and go to the ladies' room."

"Why?"

He raised one eyebrow impatiently. Was he still trying to call her bluff?

Sunnie couldn't deny it. She loved this Landon, loved the unpredictability, the macho posturing.

She lifted her wineglass, took a big swig, and then stood up.

She walked to the ladies' room and locked the door. Walking over to the mirror, she fluffed her hair and touched up her lipstick, wondering how long she should let him sweat it out at the table before returning. She was just about to head back when there was a soft knock on the door.

She unlocked the door, numbly standing aside as Landon entered and locked the door once more.

"We don't have a lot of time."

Sunnie stared at him, not realizing her mouth was hanging open until he pushed his finger below her chin, closing it.

"Your decision, Sunshine. Admit you were bluffing, that you were trying to get me to walk away from the plan—or take off your panties. Which way is this going down?"

She wished he hadn't used the words *going down*. Because she'd been on a diet a lot longer than a few months. Truth was, she'd been going hungry for more than a year, though she'd never admit that to Landon.

Sunnie had never been accused of overthinking anything.

There was a hot cop standing in front of her offering orgasms. It felt like a no-brainer.

She lifted her short skirt and tugged her panties down, kicking them off before throwing him a challenging glare. "I dare you."

It was a standard line, one the two of them had probably thrown at each other a million times in the past twenty years.

Landon was better at resisting dares than she or Finn. He was always the Boy Scout, the one to consider the consequences before acting. While she and Finn were jumping off garage roofs and eating bugs and doing countless other ridiculous, reckless things, Landon made his decision to follow through based on whether or not he thought he could do it, get away with it...or you know...not get killed.

This time, he never missed a beat, never paused. He gripped her waist, pushing her toward the sink. Once there, he turned her toward the mirror, pressed her forward over the counter, making sure she saw his face as he nudged her ankles apart with his foot, lifted her skirt, and smoothed his fingers along her slit from clit to anus.

She gasped, her head falling forward.

Landon threaded his fingers through her hair and pulled her head up until her gaze met his in the mirror.

"Don't look away. I want you to know exactly who's touching you."

She shivered at the dark, sexy-as-hell tone of his voice, even though she'd prefer to close her eyes. Facing him only reminded her who she was with and why this was a really bad idea.

"Landon," she whispered, trying to figure out if she should give this victory to him and walk away, or tell him to hurry the hell up.

He took the decision away from her, pressing two fingers inside her, straight to the hilt, as his other hand remained in her hair, the tension on her scalp turning her on in ways she couldn't begin to deal with.

Landon began thrusting his fingers in and out—first just the two, and then three. Every now and then, he'd stop, withdraw, and apply the most perfect amount of pressure to her clit. Her hips began to move, pushing back on every inward thrust. Their gazes never disconnected, and she could read the sheer determination on his face.

She'd asked for an orgasm, and by God, he fully intended to give her one.

"Unbutton the top few buttons on your blouse, Sunshine. Let me see your tits."

Sunnie reacted to the demand, wondering if he'd somehow hypnotized her. She freed the buttons, drawing the material apart to give him a bird's-eye view of her cleavage in the mirror.

He started thrusting harder, faster, and her eyes closed of their own volition as her climax approached.

"Oh my God," she gasped as her pussy clenched. She was so damn close.

"Do it, Sunnie. Come on my fingers, babe. Let me feel it. You're so tight...so goddamn tight." He followed up his amazing dirty talk with another stroke to her clit, then he sank the first knuckle of his index finger into her ass.

Sunnie was a goner. She jerked roughly, her lungs burning as she fought to hold in her cries of pleasure. She'd never been a screamer in bed, but damn...

Even out of her mind, she was vaguely cognizant of their surroundings. They were in the restroom of a very ritzy restaurant. Unfortunately, that just turned her on more.

She trembled as her orgasm started to wane. Landon's fingers disappeared, and then she heard the sound of running water as he washed his hands.

Sunnie couldn't look at him. She was too afraid to raise her eyes and see what he was thinking, how he was feeling.

She was a blob of rubber, her legs weak, her insides shivery, her heart racing.

He'd won this round.

Jesus—he might have already won the whole damn war.

Her hands were shaking slightly as she tried to rebutton her blouse. Landon pushed her hands away, taking over the task. When his fingers lightly stroked the tops of her breasts, she knew it was no accidental touch.

Her eyes, still downcast, were in the perfect position to see that he was not unaffected by what had just happened. His pants were tented with his erection—and she suddenly felt guilty.

Sunnie reached toward his pants, but Landon clasped her wrist in his firm hand. "No sex," he repeated, though his voice was gruff and the words sounded somewhat strained.

Unable to avoid it any longer, she looked up into his eyes.

And saw Landon.

Cocky bastard was grinning.

She laughed, the sound somewhat shaky. "How the hell... where did you learn to..."

Her words faded away as his eyes narrowed.

"I'm a nice guy, Sunnie. Apparently, you think that's synonymous with 'lousy in bed.' If you weren't dating gym rats hopped up on steroids all the time, you would know that's not true."

"They weren't on steroids." Then she paused, quickly adding, "Well, the lumberjack probably was."

Landon shook his head. "He definitely was. Idiot was so buff, he couldn't put his freaking arms down by his sides. Only thing he was missing was the ax."

Sunnie giggled, feeling strangely lighter and happier than she had in ages. She'd missed him the past couple of weeks.

"You haven't been around much lately," she said.

"I know. That was a mistake." He gave her a very sweet, very Landon-like kiss on the cheek, then headed for the door. He stopped and bent over to pick up her panties.

She held out her hand for them, but he shook his head, shoving them in his pocket.

"Um, those are mine, hotshot."

Landon ignored her, reaching for the doorknob. "Mine now," he said, unlocking it. Once he glanced outside to make sure no one was there, he turned back and winked at her. "Souvenir."

Sunnie laughed, tugged her skirt farther down, and then followed him back to the table.

❧ 10 ❧

"Sunnie," Landon murmured quietly, shaking her gently. "Sunnie."

She slept like the dead, so he tried again.

"Mmmm," she hummed, clearly not awake yet.

"Rise and shine, Sunshine."

Sunnie's hair was a tangled mess on the pillow, the covers twisted in a pretzel. She slept on her stomach, arms stretched upwards, diagonally on the queen-size mattress.

Sunnie and Yvonne had shared a bedroom up until about a year ago when their older cousins Caitlyn and Ailis moved in with their boyfriends. That left an extra room, so Yvonne claimed it. Sunnie, delighted to have more space, immediately traded in the single bed for a queen. He knew that because it had been he and Finn who'd lugged the old bed out and the new one in.

She wore an oversized T-shirt and boxers.

"Sunnie," he tried again, sitting on the side of the mattress, shaking her a bit harder.

She blinked a few times, and he suspected she was trying to focus.

"Landon?"

"Yeah. You need to get up, babe."

She glanced around her room, confused. He didn't blame her. He'd dropped her off last night after their dinner date, only walking her as far as the entrance to the pub, where he'd given her a pretty legit good-night kiss.

She thought it had been for the benefit of the dozen or so tabloid photographers there. He knew it was for him.

"What time is it?" she mumbled, her voice husky from sleep. She was still trying to function.

"Six."

She frowned, and for the first time it looked like she was fully conscious. "As in a.m.?"

He nodded.

"What the hell are you doing here?"

"I have a key. I've always had one."

Her frown was more scowl as she said, "I know that, jackass. I didn't ask how you got *in* here. I asked why you're here. In my room. At the ass crack of dawn. I'm on vacation. That means sleeping in."

"One of the producers from a local news show called me and said they had a last-minute cancellation this morning. He was hoping you and I could make an appearance. Nothing major. We just go on and answer a few questions. Whole segment isn't going to last more than five minutes."

She sat up, tugging at the leg of her boxers. He was sorry she'd done that. One side had ridden up, giving him ample view of her entire thigh and the tiniest bit of her ass cheek.

"Are you serious?"

"Yeah. I thought you'd be excited. It's that *New Day Baltimore* thing with the hot weather guy. You love that show."

"Well, I do, but...what are we going to say?"

"That's why I'm here early. I thought you could get a quick shower, then we'll grab some breakfast, get our stories straight. Our segment airs live at nine-fifty, but the guy would like us there an hour early for makeup and to briefly go over things."

Landon had expected her to jump right on this, but she still hesitated. "Why would you agree to this? You're going to hate every minute of it."

He shrugged. He was. He *really* was. But he knew she'd love it—even now he could see she was starting to get excited by the prospect—and it gave him the chance to further his cause. Finn and Sunnie had both mentioned that their fifteen minutes of fame would fade soon, and they were right.

Which meant Landon needed to make the most of the time he had if he hoped to achieve his dream.

He had one goal right now—and it was to win Sunnie's heart.

That required finesse, skill and outright subterfuge. She'd never go down easy, so he would just have to trick her, seduce her into it. Last night had been a pretty hot start. He'd jerked off three times since as he recalled the way her face flushed when she came on his fingers.

Landon stood up, offering her a hand. "I figured you could do the majority of the talking."

Sunnie obviously didn't have a problem with that. But that didn't mean there *wasn't* a problem as she leapt out of bed and darted to the closet. "Dammit! What the hell am I going to wear?"

He chuckled, following her. After a twenty-minute discussion of her wardrobe, Sunnie went to the bathroom for a shower while he meandered to the kitchen. He was just polishing off the bagel with cream cheese he'd helped himself to when she appeared.

"I thought we were going to breakfast."

"That was just an appetizer. Daily Grind?"

She nodded and they headed downstairs. Her uncles Tris and Ewan were sitting at the counter of the bar, having a cup of coffee, discussing last night's ball game. They hadn't been there when Landon arrived, which made things awkward...and potentially dangerous. Her uncles were big guys and protective of their nieces...and sisters...and wives...and daughters.

"Late night or early morning?" Tris asked.

Sunnie gave both of her uncles a quick kiss on the cheek. Now that she'd showered and dressed, she'd come fully to life, the excitement over her television interview growing by the minute.

"We're going to be on TV," she said, filling them in on the details—the channel, show and time. "Talking about our viral video."

Ewan was amused by Sunnie's enthusiasm. "We'll be sure to watch it."

They started to leave, but Sunnie turned around just as they reached the door. "Oh, I almost forgot. Landon and I are pretending to be a couple to scare away all the single ladies who've been swarming since his Hot Cop debut. Do not become alarmed," she said casually. "It's all make believe."

Sunnie turned away, not noticing the narrowed-eyed, suspicious looks her uncles shot in his direction. He gave them a subtle one-shouldered shrug, then turned to follow Sunnie.

They walked hand in hand to the coffee shop. There were no cameras, no fawning women, no one watching. There was no one on the street with them besides people rushing to work, so he didn't need to hold her hand.

But he wanted to. Mercifully, Sunnie didn't give him shit for it or try to pull away.

Once they got their coffee and breakfast sandwiches, they found a table in a quiet corner.

"I suspect they'll ask about our relationship, so I was thinking—" Sunnie started, her eyes bright. If he knew her—and he did—she was ready to concoct the mother of all stories, something over-the-top and probably ridiculous.

Landon headed her off at the pass. "I was too," he interjected. "The safest, smartest bet is sticking as closely to the truth as possible."

Her shoulders slumped and it was clear she didn't care for that suggestion. Regardless, he pressed on. "We just say we've known each other since we were kids. After the mugging, we realized our feelings had changed from just friends to something more."

She feigned a yawn. "Oh, I'm sorry. What did you say?" she said sarcastically. "I fell asleep halfway through that thrilling tale of our romance."

Landon closed his eyes, pretending to be annoyed. It was a look he'd perfected over the years, simply because he'd seen it repeated on Aaron's and Finn's faces so often. The Young men had a patented look whenever Riley or Sunnie or Darcy said or did something outrageous. And they, like him, used it to hide the fact that rather than exasperated, they were entertained.

The Young women had an energy, a love for life that was undeniably fun. Landon used to laugh at Sunnie's antics, until Finn insisted it only encouraged her to go even wilder. Somewhere along the line, Landon had chosen his side, crossed over and joined the men, adopting their fake impatience.

"We're not making up some asinine story, Sunnie. For one thing, too many people know us and someone, somewhere, would contradict it. And for another, we don't have time for it. We're going on air in just a couple of hours."

"Landon—" she started.

"Nonnegotiable."

She leaned back and crossed her arms, though he didn't think she looked angry as much as confused. "So our story is we've been friends forever, you kissed me after the mugging, and that was it? It was a lights-on moment and now we're head over heels?"

From her tone, Sunnie seemed to think that concept implausible.

Landon knew better. Except his lights turned on at the April Fools party.

"Why do you find that so hard to believe?" he asked.

"Because we *do* know each other so well. If we were going to fall in love, it wouldn't have been because of a kiss—or two kisses," she corrected, recalling the April Fools party.

"How many kisses do you need to know you're in love with someone?" It would have been a practical question if he'd been asking anyone besides Sunnie. But he knew her dating track record. She reminded him of the damn Tootsie Pop owl. She didn't know how many kisses because she'd give a guy three licks, then crunch. End of the line.

She shrugged. "More than two."

Sunnie was very good at saying things with absolute confidence. It gave people around her this misguided sense that she actually knew what she was talking about.

"How many?" he pressed, calling her on it. No guy had ever pushed the envelope with her. Primarily because she only accepted dates with men whose biceps were bigger than their brains. None of her previous boyfriends had challenged her, forced the issue of feelings and commitment because they were shallow vessels.

Sunnie was smart enough to know that, so she'd found the perfect way to guard her heart.

There was a small part inside him that thought he should have his head examined for even thinking about dating Sunnie, simply because he had a healthy dose of self-preservation himself, and he had no idea how this was going to end up.

All he knew was what he wanted.

Her. Forever.

However, her confidence was only overshadowed by her stubbornness. She wouldn't go down without a fight.

"A ton of kisses. Close to a million."

Landon shook his head and made a buzzer sound to indicate he was calling her on her bullshit. "Nope. I'm going to need a more practical answer."

"How many times did you kiss Audrey before some 'ah-ha, I'm in love' moment?" It was a classic duck and cover move on her part. If she didn't know the answer, she changed the subject, putting the questioner on the offensive instead.

"Four times."

She snorted before she realized he was serious.

"Four times," she repeated. "That sounds like you. You are a hopeless romantic, Landon. What happened to make it the fourth the one?"

"You've already heard my Audrey stories, Sunnie." She, like Finn, had been his confidante the past seven or eight years. Typically, it was the three of them at the bar, talking about relationships, sports, future plans. She had been his friend every step of the way through the Audrey years.

"Never in this context. I mean, I heard about the dates and the getting-lucky parts. And I was there when she left." Her eyes softened.

Landon had been brokenhearted when Audrey realized she would regret not taking her shot at Broadway if she settled down with him in Baltimore. He'd respected her honesty even though it had shattered him.

The night she'd thrown her stuff in the back of her car and taken off for the bright lights of the big city, Finn and Sunnie had shown up, armed with pizza and beer, and they'd cued up every John Cusack movie on Finn's iTunes account. Sunnie's brother had a serious man-crush on John Cusack for some reason.

"Our first date was a blind date, set up by one of the guys at the precinct. The second was a work function, summer picnic. She hung out with the other wives and girlfriends and taught three little girls how to play hopscotch after drawing the boxes out with sidewalk chalk for them."

"And the third," she continued for him, "was the two of you walking along the Inner Harbor for hours, just holding hands and talking, amazed by how much you had in common." She said it in a dreamy, faraway voice, teasing him for what she perceived was a flaw. Only Sunnie would see romance as a shortcoming.

Of course, she wasn't wrong about the third date, which just proved to him she'd been paying attention more than he realized to his relationship with Audrey.

Rather than give her the point, he joked, "I swear to God you were dropped on your head as a baby. It's the only thing that could explain you growing up with Aaron and Riley and thinking romance is cheesy."

She laughed. "Probably. So what was this magical fourth date?"

"We met you and Finn and a bunch of other Collinses at the pub for karaoke."

"Oh yeah. I remember that night."

"She fit in, thought all of you were awesome. We left at closing time and we were walking toward my car. She kept going on and on about what a great family you were and...I kissed her. And I knew—thought—she was the woman I was going to spend the rest of my life with. She was fine with my job, good with kids, said she wanted to get married, rooted for all the same sports teams, watched all the same TV shows, and she loved all of you."

"That sort of sounds like a checklist."

It did, but he hadn't thought of it that way until he'd said it all out loud. "I guess it does."

"Wow. That might be the least romantic thing you've ever said."

Landon nodded, feeling slightly off-balance. He'd spent months after Audrey left feeling as if he was trying to rebound from a broken heart. Now it seemed as if that depression was based more on *what* he'd lost, not *who* he'd lost. "I think it is."

"It's that marriage problem of yours."

"Problem?" he asked.

"You want a wife and kids like...yesterday."

"I don't think that's a problem, Sunnie."

"Hear me out," she continued. "It was just you and your mom, pretty much your whole life. That had to be quiet and lonely. Then you'd come over to our house, where it was noise and chaos and insanity, and for some weird reason, you liked that. A lot."

"I did...do. I don't think it's any secret I look up to your dad. I look at his life and I know it's what I want. More than that, he's the kind of man I want to be. He was always really good to me, Sunnie. I was starving for a guy to pay attention to me, to toss the ball around, even just to give me hell for failing my spelling test."

"You're a shit speller."

He grinned, even though he couldn't quite figure out what her point was. "What's wrong with wanting to live a life like Aaron Young?"

"Not a damn thing," she said quickly. "If you manage that, you'll have a pretty freaking great life. I just..." She sighed. "I just hope you let it happen naturally. I'm pretty sure my dad didn't have a perfect wife checklist, and I can promise you, if he did, Mom didn't check one single box. She struggled—hell, she *still* struggles—with his job, she's way more social than he is, constantly dragging him to places he doesn't want to go, and while they both wanted kids, Mom wanted eight, but Dad put his foot down at three. Personally, I blame Darcy. She was a handful."

Landon gave her a look that said he wasn't going there because they both knew the truth. Darcy had been the perfect baby.

Sunnie continued, completely oblivious to what she was doing—solidifying something that was becoming more obvious by the second. "Just make sure you pick a woman based on the right reasons. Audrey might have checked all the boxes, but I'm not sure that made her the one. You know what I mean?"

Landon nodded. "I know exactly what you mean."

He loved Sunnie.

She was imperfectly perfect for him.

"Cool," she said, clueless to what she'd just unleashed.

Landon glanced at the time on his phone. "We better get going."

She took his hand this time, winking at what she considered great acting. He squeezed it fondly and they left the coffee shop.

Two hours later, Landon found himself sitting on a couch with Sunnie on the set of the morning show. She'd been right. He hated sitting in front of the cameras, under the lights. He felt like a jackass.

Landon had turned down countless requests for interviews, but he'd decided to bite the bullet on this one because he knew it was one of Sunnie's favorite shows. And given the grin on her face, she definitely loved every minute of it.

Mercifully, he hadn't had to say more than a few words as Sunnie took the lead. Not that this interview would help him at work. He would never live this down.

She was sticking to the truth, as they'd discussed, claiming that kiss changed everything between them. Sunnie didn't realize exactly how accurate that was.

The anchorwoman, Beverly Monroe, sounded far too much like the women who'd written him love letters, constantly batting her eyes at him, flushing whenever he looked her direction, giggling at the two comments he'd made, even though neither had been particularly funny.

"I imagine," Beverly said to Sunnie, "it became pretty obvious how Landon felt about you right after that kiss. The way he looked at you was..." The woman sighed for dramatic effect. "So dreamy! Every woman in the world wants to be looked at like that, am I right?"

For the first time, Sunnie faltered, clearly confused, her grin appearing frozen in place. It took a few seconds before she managed an unconvincing nod, and Landon wondered what was going on.

The cameraman gave Beverly a signal, music started playing as she closed the show. Once it was over, she thanked both of them for coming, shaking Landon's hand a little longer than was probably polite.

Sunnie's eyes narrowed briefly before she gave him a subtle, exasperated eye roll behind Beverly's back.

They gathered their stuff and headed for the car. There were about twenty women standing outside the studio, and they pressed forward when he and Sunnie emerged. It took them a good ten minutes before they were able to push themselves free.

Once they were in the car, Sunnie said, "I get it."

"Get what?"

"I've only really been dealing with tabloid photographers, who, while annoying, don't invade my personal space like that. Did that one woman really just grab your ass?"

The woman had, her hand slipping away quickly when Landon turned, piercing her with his don't-fuck-with-me cop face.

"Yeah. But on the plus side, there were fewer than before. First day after my name was released, I think there were close to seventy-five women outside the precinct."

"Holy shit. I had no idea how crazy they've been."

Landon pulled out of the parking garage, still bothered by Sunnie's face at the end of the show. His gut was telling him that something didn't make sense.

When Beverly had mentioned his face in the video, Landon realized she was perplexed—that she didn't seem to know what the woman was referring to.

"Sunnie, have you seen the video of us?"

She appeared surprised—and then unnerved—by his question. And his suspicion was confirmed.

"Of course I have."

"How many times?"

She turned away from him, looking out the passenger window. "I don't know. Why does that matter?"

"How many times?" he pressed.

Sunnie did her usual duck and cover. "How many times have

*you* seen it?"

"Too many. Fucking Miguel pulls it up on his iPad pretty much hourly at work, doing this running commentary for anyone who will listen." It was one reason Landon wasn't surprised by Beverly's comment about the look. It was Miguel's favorite part of the video, the place he always paused and made sure to point out Landon's million-dollar heartthrob moment.

Miguel had mistaken it for some sexy move on Landon's part.

Landon now recognized it as something different.

Love.

Sunnie giggled. "I'll have to get Miguel to do the color commentary for me."

"How many times, Sunnie?"

She faced him, annoyed. "Landon."

He waited at a stoplight, the red light giving him a chance to look at her, to show her he wasn't going to let the subject drop.

"Once," she admitted quietly.

Landon frowned. "One time? You've only seen it once?"

"I was there," she said, her words a weak defense. "I saw it all in person. Why do I need to watch the video?"

He didn't have a clue what to make of that confession. Sunnie had approached the whole viral thing with an unbridled enthusiasm, enjoying the limelight.

So why wouldn't she embrace the video that brought her that fame?

Sunnie's gaze darted away a split second before the light turned green. The reaction told him exactly why she hadn't watched it.

She was afraid.

What he *didn't* know was what had spooked her.

The kiss?

The look?

Or had she realized the same thing as him?

That nothing between them was make-believe, and he would never think of Sunnie as a sister ever again.

❧ I I ❧

Landon sat on a padded chair on the sidelines of the high school gym where the charity basketball game was about to start, looking hotter than any man had the right to in gray Under Armour shorts and a navy-blue T-shirt.

He hadn't seen her yet, which gave Sunnie a minute to try to get this strange initial reaction to him under control. She'd noticed that every day since they'd started pretending to be a couple, there was this brief period of honest-to-God nervousness right before he arrived at the pub to pick her up. It was an insane feeling, considering it was Landon who was making her feel so...twittery.

It was the only word she could come up with to describe it.

Pushing that aside, she fluffed her hair and turned to Yvonne. "You ready for our grand entrance?"

Yvonne nodded, while Jessica, one of the nurses from the hospital, tried to tug down her skirt and said, "We should have told them we were planning to do this."

Sunnie grinned. "Ruins the surprise if you warn people."

Yvonne laughed as Sunnie led her squad into the gymnasium.

Both teams had just claimed their half of the floor for warm-ups when the cheerleaders entered.

Sunnie had managed to come up with six uniforms and Aunt Lane had helped her emblazon three of them with the Baltimore police emblem, the other three with the firefighters'. They shook their pom-poms, lining up on the end of the court where Landon and his cop buddies were taking turns shooting layups.

Landon froze mid-shot, nearly falling down when Miguel, who hadn't seen them yet, ran into him, expecting him to shoot and move.

"What the hell, man?" Miguel said before spotting them. "Sweet Jesus. My high school wet dreams just came to life."

Landon dropped the ball, walking toward her. Sunnie gave him a pretty decent herkie, shaking her pom-poms as she did so.

"We thought the game could use a cheer squad," she said as he got closer.

He didn't acknowledge her comment with words or a wave. Instead, he just kept coming.

Gripping her by the waist, he pulled her to him and gave her a kiss that definitely would have gotten both of them sent to the principal's office if they were really in high school.

It took a second before either of them heard the whistle that continued to grow louder. Landon released her two seconds before her dad—the coach—gave him a slap to the back of the head.

"What the hell are you doing, boy? We got our asses handed to us last year by the firefighters. I don't intend to lose again. Get out there, warmup, and pay attention to the ball!"

Landon returned to the court, but from the constant glances he kept shooting over his shoulder, she wouldn't say his head was in the game.

"Sunnie, Yvonne," Dad said. "You look great, but I'm telling you right now, if you distract my team, I'm sending you out of here."

"Dad—" Sunnie started.

Her father grinned as he leaned closer. "Have mercy on poor Landon."

He walked away as Yvonne stepped next to her. "That guy has got it *bad* for you."

Sunnie shook her head, trying to disregard her family's nonchalant attitude to her and Landon and all these pretend— why didn't they feel like pretend?—kisses. She didn't want to think about what any of that might mean.

Especially considering Landon had actually pulled back since that interview, kissing her only in public and not initiating any more of his killer orgasms.

Not that she'd asked for them.

She'd barely held it together at the end of that damn TV interview, not sure how to respond to Beverly's comment about the way Landon had looked at her in the video. It was the same thing Pop Pop had said, and it had freaked her out.

Sometime during the ride home from the television station, it felt as if they'd both sort of realized they shouldn't cross the line anymore. So...it had been nine days of nothing but fake dates, hand-holding and tame good-night kisses.

Sunnie had hated every minute of the...platonicness—she didn't care if that wasn't a word. So she'd come up with the cheerleader idea. Smart or not, Sunnie was going back in for another orgasm. Her brain had been overruled by her vagina, and the diet ended today. With any luck, it would be a spectacular cheat.

The game started, so Sunnie and the police half of her squad claimed the first row of the bleachers, standing up whenever the score got tight to lead the police department fans in a cheer. The other half went to cheer for the firefighters. Twice they'd started a wave that made it all the way around the gymnasium.

At halftime, the firefighters were up by two. Typically, halftime was a ten-minute break where the coaches for each team gave their players a pep talk from the sidelines, and the fans just socialized or purchased baked goods donated to add more money to the charitable contribution. This year, Sunnie had something special planned. She glanced over her shoulder and spotted Finn in the press box. The announcer for the game handed him the microphone.

"Ladies and gentlemen," Finn said, pausing as everyone got quiet. "As you know, we're here today for a very good cause. All the money raised will be contributed directly to the Children's Cancer Foundation. Today, we have a special treat for all you fans. Our nursing cheer squad has prepared a special halftime show. Put your hands to together for the nurses...and Yvonne," he added, as everyone laughed.

Unbeknownst to Landon, she and the nurses had spent the better part of four days getting ready for this, practicing on every break they had at work. Last night, they'd done a dress rehearsal for the kids in the pediatric oncology ward and, despite a few missteps, they'd been a hit, the kids laughing, singing, and dancing as much as they were able. Her nursing supervisor warned her they'd want an encore every week. Sunnie assured her that wouldn't be a hardship at all.

Sunnie ran toward the middle of the floor, nailing her round-off. Jessica managed a pretty decent cartwheel, and damned if Yvonne didn't sink down into a legit split. Once they'd all made it to their places, she looked at Finn, who gave her a thumbs-up. Then the music started.

Sunnie made sure she was watching Landon when the first few notes of the song came on, and she laughed the second he recognized it and rolled his eyes.

*High School Musical* had been Sunnie's jam for the better part of middle school. She'd seen the movie—and sequels—no less than a thousand times, and she knew the original movie's show-ending dance number by heart.

She had roped Finn and Landon into learning it with her one summer when they were all bored, and while both boys grumbled, they'd given her the better part of an afternoon, and then agreed to perform a "show" for their parents, Pop Pop and Bubbles after dinner that night.

When the chorus to "We're All in This Together" came on, Sunnie, Yvonne and the nurses started the routine, all of them laughing when Miguel ran from the sidelines to join them. Miguel had gone out with them maybe a dozen times over the course of the last year, ever since he'd moved to Baltimore and joined the force. He was great fun and easy to be around, but when he started dancing and proved he knew every single step, Sunnie decided right then and there, he was going to be her best friend forever.

Glancing up, she saw Finn doing a few of the moves in the press box, feeling secure that no one was looking at him. During the turn, she realized Finn wasn't completely unnoticed.

Miguel was watching her brother too.

Then she looked at Landon, standing relatively still on the sidelines, his eyes locked on her. When she threw him a wink and raised one eyebrow in challenge, he lifted his hands to do the wildcat scratch in time with the song.

Oh yeah. He remembered it.

Of course, unlike Miguel, who was relishing the cheers and attention, Landon was content to just watch her.

"Those are my babies!" Sunnie heard Bubbles yell from the bleachers. A quick peek in that direction proved her entire family was on their feet, bouncing in time to the music, laughing and cheering them on. Even Pop Pop was doing a little shuffle, reaching over to grab Darcy's hand and give her a spin in place.

They got a standing ovation once the song ended.

Landon started to walk toward her, but before he got there, she felt a hand slide over her eyes, a deep male voice murmuring, "You look hot in that skirt."

Sunnie pulled the hand away and turned, surprised to see Naked Ned standing there. She and Ned had dated a few years earlier, the relationship lasting almost five months, which put him at the top of the list in terms of longest boyfriend.

"Ned. What are you doing here?"

"My cousin is playing for the firefighters. I got here halfway through first half. Thought that was you sitting across the court."

Her family and Landon had nicknamed him Naked Ned one night after they'd all gone club-hopping together. Ned had come back to the apartment with her, the two of them turning in early. At some point, Ned—sans clothes—had decided to venture to the kitchen for a snack. Finn, Landon, Colm and Padraig had still been awake. Apparently, Ned hadn't felt any compunction in having a conversation with the four of them, his balls swinging in the breeze. The chat had ended when Sunnie had come out, spotted him, and asked why the hell he was naked.

The nickname stuck, but Ned was gone before dawn the next morning.

"Yeah, I'm here cheering for my dad's team."

The buzzer sounded to announce the end of halftime. Sunnie looked over her shoulder to find Landon staring at her. Miguel slapped him on the shoulder to grab his attention, and Landon took his spot on the court as she and Ned walked to the sidelines.

"It's good to see you," Ned said, his gaze sliding up and down. It took everything Sunnie had not to roll her eyes at his ogling.

Guys and cheerleaders. So typical.

"You too." She endured a few minutes of small talk as Ned chatted about his job, hinting strongly that he was newly single again.

"Sunnie!"

She turned at the sound of her dad calling her name. She spotted him standing on the sidelines, hands on his hips, scowling. Then he jerked his head toward the court where Landon was playing...badly. One eye on the basket, the other on her. A quick glance at the scoreboard told her the cops were now down by six.

"Duty calls," she said to Ned, grateful for the chance to get away from him.

"Maybe we can—"

"We can't," she said, heading him off at the pass. "I'm dating Landon."

She saw the look of surprise on his face and tamped down her annoyance that Ned seemed to consider that relationship so unlikely.

Sunnie sat next to Yvonne, who said, "If looks could kill, Ned would be a chalk outline on the floor right now."

"Very funny," Sunnie murmured, secretly pleased to think Landon was jealous.

She shoved that pleasure away when she realized that was actually a bad thing.

Jesus.

She was twenty kinds of fucked-up right now.

With her safely back on the cops' side of the gym, Ned on the other, Landon turned on the heat, nailing back-to-back three pointers in the last quarter to propel his team to victory.

Dad had appointed Landon team captain, though neither of them was sure if that was a nod to Hot Cop, or as punishment for all the shit that viral video caused. As a result, a reporter from the newspaper, there to write about the game, pulled him aside as the rest of the team headed to the locker room.

Sunnie hung back with her family, chatting for a little while as the crowd thinned. When it looked like the interview was wrapping up, she started to approach him.

Two other women beat her there. Sunnie hadn't noticed them hovering on the sidelines, but it was clear they were part of the Hot Cop fan club.

"You got a ride, Sunnie?" Dad asked.

She'd come with Yvonne, but her cousin had left right after the third quarter because she was waiting tables at the pub tonight and needed to shower.

"Yeah," she lied. "Landon is bringing me home."

Dad glanced at Landon chatting with the two women and

gave her a curious look. She was relieved when—rather than question her about it—he simply nodded and said goodbye.

She walked toward Landon and the women, surprised that, rather than trying to get away from them—as he had every other overzealous groupie who'd approached him since they'd started to pretend date—he was actually taking part in the conversation.

Sunnie saw red when he smiled at the very pretty blonde, laughing at something she said.

"You ready to go, Landon?" Sunnie asked, grasping his hand and tucking herself close to his side. He'd told her she was going to be a jealous girlfriend, part of her job description when he had proposed this plan. She dismissed the other women with barely a glance, intent on pulling him away.

Landon actually shot her a surprised look and didn't budge. "Sunnie," he said, wrapping his arm around her waist to hold her still. He glanced around the gym, then pierced her with a look that seemed...angry. "Where's Ned?"

His question sparked her own temper. How dare he play high and mighty with her when he was standing here flirting with two women?

"Gone."

"Um, hi, Sunnie."

Sunnie was taken aback when the blonde said her name, then she recognized her as a girl who'd gone to high school with her and Landon. "Cathy."

"I was just telling Landon how happy I am that the two of you are finally going out." Cathy reached over and took the other woman's hand. "My girlfriend wanted to meet the two of you. We figured you're as close to famous as we're going to get here in Baltimore."

The two women grinned. They were clearly in love...and it was obvious now that they'd merely wanted to say hello.

Sunnie felt bad for her possessive behavior. "I would hardly call us famous. How have you been?"

They chatted for a few minutes as Sunnie tried to get her

emotions under control. Landon didn't seem to be doing any better than she. He radiated heat and his arm tightened around her waist, his fingers gripping her in an unbreakable hold.

Cathy and her girlfriend said goodbye, leaving the gym...and Landon and Sunnie alone.

"Landon," Sunnie said, trying to shrug out of his hold.

"Not one word, Sunnie."

"What?" she asked, surprised by his tone.

Landon grasped her hand and tugged her from the gym and into the nearest locker room. The other guys had already showered and left, the place empty.

He pressed her back against a row of lockers and kissed her as if his life depended on it.

She returned the heated embrace, nipping at his lower lip, causing him to jerk back and, holy shit, *growl*.

Sunnie gripped his hair, pulling his face back to hers. As they kissed, his hands drifted under her sweater, his fingers roughly pulling her bra down until her breasts popped free. He pinched her nipples, causing her to gasp, their lips parting.

"You have no idea what that sweater is doing to me."

"Cheerleader fetish much?" She was trying for a joke, reaching for some way to calm down. It didn't work. Especially when he pinched her nipples again.

"What did Ned want?"

She snarled. "Nothing. Just saying hi."

"He didn't ask you out?"

Sunnie was in over her head, still irrationally angry at him for talking to Cathy and her girlfriend. Knowing the women were lesbians and not flirting with Landon wasn't helping.

"None of your business."

He ripped her sweater over her head in one swoop, sucking one of her nipples into his mouth. He pulled on the tight nub until she saw stars. Her pussy clenched hungrily.

Landon released her with a pop, his face coming up until their lips were a mere inch away. "We have a deal."

"Funny," she said. "I don't remember any orgasms this past week."

"You're playing with fire, babe."

"Maybe I should find one of the firefighters to help me out," she taunted, her gaze drifting to the front of his pants, tented with his erection. She was out of control, spiraling.

She didn't care.

Her fingers lightly grazed his dick before he gripped her wrist, holding her hand away. "Sunnie, if you touch me…"

He didn't finish his comment, didn't need to.

They were so far over the line, they were in another state right now.

But she'd never been accused of being too bright, and this was no exception. She shook off his grip, running her hand over his cock. He sucked in a hard breath.

His loose-fitting pants made it easy for her to cup his hard length.

Twenty years of friendship and she'd had no idea Landon was…so well-endowed.

"Holy shit," she whispered.

"You have to let go, Sunnie, or this isn't going to end the way you want," he said, kissing the side of her neck. His breath was hot, he was rock-hard, and she'd never been more turned on in her life.

"I…can't."

"Dammit," he murmured. He pulled her hand away, lifting it and the other next to her head, pressing them against the locker. "One of these days, you're going to have to learn self-control."

She grinned, the return of his normal Landon voice, exasperated with her, easing the tension.

"I'm sorry," she murmured, grateful for his strength in the face of whatever the fuck this was. "God, I'm sorry. I keep going too far."

He kissed her cheek. "I'm sorry too."

She tilted her head, smiled. "It's okay—" she started.

"No. Not for that. I'm sorry for this."

He lifted her skirt and ran his hand down the front of her panties, damp with her arousal.

"Landon," she gasped, as he dropped to his knees in front of her, reaching for the elastic and tugging her panties down. He pulled them over her sneakers, then lifted one leg, pulling her knee over his shoulder.

"Oh my God!" she called out when he drew her clit into his mouth and sucked hard. Sunnie's hands flew to his head, her fingers gripping his hair. His beard tickled her inner thighs. "Please," she whispered. "More."

He gave her what she wanted, thrusting two fingers inside her as he nipped at her clit.

Sunnie's heart pounded, her body racing toward the quickest orgasm of her life. Landon had gotten her ninety percent of the way with just his words and his possessive kisses.

He pressed a third finger in—and she came loudly, quivering from head to toe.

Landon leaned back, his ass resting on his heels as he looked up, as surprised as she was by her almost-immediate climax.

She was still reeling, still trying to pull herself back to reality, when he stood up.

"We're going back to my place," he announced. Again with the heavy-handed proclamations.

"Okay," she agreed.

She was a fool.

## 12

Landon pushed her against the closed door of his apartment and kissed her.

Sunnie's hands wrapped around his neck, her breasts pressed tight against his chest.

If he'd been capable of reason, of thinking, Landon wouldn't be here. That much he knew.

He'd come up with a game plan, knew that taking Sunnie would change everything. Until he was certain of her heart, he couldn't risk so much.

That was what his head and his heart knew.

Unfortunately, his dick was in control. And it wanted something else.

Especially when one of Sunnie's hands drifted lower, slipping beneath the elastic and finding him hard, ready.

She ran her fist up and down the erect flesh half a dozen or so times before he stepped back, out of her grip. He was too fucking close, and he refused to come undone in her hand like some horny teenaged boy.

"Get on the couch."

She hadn't bothered to put her panties back on after their brief interlude in the locker room. He hadn't given her the opportunity. Instead, he'd scooped them up and tossed them into his gym bag.

She'd given him a stern look and told him she wasn't going to have any panties left if he kept stealing them. He'd simply said, "If I had my way, you'd never wear them again."

Then she'd flashed him a look that said she wouldn't mind giving them up for him.

At that point, any chance he'd had at stopping this runaway train had vanished. They'd walked to his car and he'd told her to pull her skirt up and spread her legs for him. Then he'd told her to play with herself as he drove, sneaking way too many peeks.

Jesus. Talk about distracted driving.

Especially when her cheeks flushed and her breathing became labored. If he'd lived a few minutes farther away from the school, she probably would have managed to make herself come again.

But they'd arrived here too soon. He had lucked into a spot on the road, right in front of his building.

And now...now he was about to do the dumbest—and smartest—thing in his life.

He was going to fuck Sunnie Young.

And make love to her.

At the same time.

Because he wanted both things from her.

Sunnie sat on the couch, then lay on her back, crooking her finger at him.

While he was torn in a million different pieces, it was clear Sunnie was all systems go.

Typical.

Here he was analyzing and dissecting and worrying.

And he knew Sunnie would do all that too.

Afterwards.

He walked toward the couch. Right or wrong, he was only human, and pretending this wasn't real this past week or so had taken its toll on him.

Nothing had ever felt more real in his life.

Sunnie lifted her skirt, baring her pussy to him as her legs parted.

He'd tasted her in the locker room. He wanted more.

Kneeling at the end of the couch, he lifted her legs, resting her knees on his shoulders as he licked her slit, her arousal tangy on his tongue.

Sunnie's hips jerked toward his lips when he took another swipe.

"Landon!" she cried, her tone breathless, hungry. "Please."

He lifted his head, grinning at her. Her eyes clouded, confused, until he said, "I like when you beg."

Then they narrowed.

Landon didn't bother to take heed. "Get ready to do a lot more of that." He lowered his head again, cutting off any disparaging remark she might make by sucking her clit into his mouth.

"Oh my God," she said. Her fingers gripped his hair, tugging it.

Landon lifted her up, his hands on her bare ass cheeks, as he dipped his tongue inside her, thrusting several times.

Sunnie gasped, calling his name over and over. Finally, she gave him exactly what he wanted.

Unbridled begging.

"Please, Landon. God, please. I need you! Need..."

He pushed himself up, still kneeling between her legs. He pulled off his shirt, then shoved his shorts down, standing briefly to pull them off completely.

Sunnie reacted before he could return to the couch, sitting up, gripping his cock in her hands, licking the underside.

Now it was his turn to fist *her* hair, pull it, as her lips parted and she took him inside her mouth.

Her breath was hot, rapid. She was on the edge. From the blowjob?

God, how had she been standing right in front of him his

entire life and he'd never seen her, never realized that she was the one for him?

The only one.

Sunnie fisted the base of his cock, stroking the part that wouldn't fit in her mouth with her strong grip. The head of his dick touched the back of her throat, then she swallowed.

"Fuck." He used his grip in her hair to pull her mouth away.

Sunnie tried to resume her position, but he shook his head.

"Lay back down."

His words penetrated, and she returned to her previous position as he came over her, caging her beneath him.

She wrapped her legs around his waist, her hand guiding him to her wet opening.

He knew Sunnie was on the pill. She had been since she was seventeen. He could still recall the first time Finn had realized that, coming across the pink packet of pills in her nightstand drawer one day when he was looking for spare batteries Sunnie had told him were there. She hadn't remembered what else was tucked there as well.

Their parents hadn't been home, and she and Landon had been sitting in the living room, waiting for him to return with the batteries for the DVD remote.

Finn had tossed the pills on her lap, asking her what the hell those were for. When she'd rolled her eyes, dissing his overprotective older brother routine, Finn had lost it, claiming she was too young for sex.

What would Finn say when he found out about *this*?

Landon shoved that thought aside as he pressed the head of his cock just inside her. He paused, his gaze capturing hers.

It was too soon for this.

She wasn't ready for what he wanted. Everything he wanted.

He thought he saw that same glimmer of panic reflected in her eyes when she looked at him.

Then, dammit, she smiled...an easygoing, pretty, purely Sunnie smile.

Landon lowered his head and kissed her, then—

There was a knock at the door.

They lay there, frozen, the head of his dick no more than an inch inside her.

Sunnie's chest rose and fell rapidly, drawing his attention to her breasts, still hidden beneath her cheerleading sweater.

Neither of them spoke.

Then there was another knock. "Landon," Finn called from the corridor. "Open up, man. I know you're home. I saw your car outside."

Her brother's voice had the effect of someone dumping a bucket of ice water on them. Sunnie scrambled to push him off her, sitting up and tugging her skirt down. She was shaking her head slightly, as if trying to come out of some sort of spell.

Landon moved away, sitting on the couch. He was naked and his erection was pointing skyward. He didn't want to consider the case of blue balls he was going to suffer for this.

"Give me a minute," Landon called out when Finn knocked a third time.

He rubbed his eyes wearily, opening them when Sunnie moved closer, her hand cupping his jaw, pulling until he looked at her.

"I'm sorry," she whispered.

He frowned. "Not your fault. I...we're... Finn and I have tickets to the Orioles game tonight. I forgot."

SUNNIE STRUGGLED TO CATCH HER BREATH. "WE ALMOST LET that go too far. We shouldn't have done that."

He didn't respond, not with words, not with a single nod or shake of his head. Instead, he just looked at her, and she fought to figure out what he was thinking.

"Say something," she urged when the silence dragged on.

Landon moved forward, placing his forehead against hers. "There are a lot of things I've done in my life that I shouldn't have," he admitted, though Sunnie doubted that. Landon was too thoughtful to act carelessly. "This wasn't one of them."

"This is all still pretend, right?"

Landon sighed, his face unreadable.

Finally, he nodded. Just a nod. No words.

Landon had never lied to her. Not once in her life.

Until now.

"I'm going to get a shower," he said, kissing her softly on the cheek. "You let him in."

She nodded numbly.

"We'll talk later, Sunnie. I promise," he said. "There isn't time now. Not with Finn standing outside. The longer we stall, the harder this is going to be to explain."

He was right. "Okay."

Sunnie watched Landon disappear into the bathroom, waiting until she heard the water running. Then she stood on unsteady legs, smoothed out her sweater and skirt and opened the door.

Finn frowned when he saw her there, clearly expecting Landon. "Sunnie? What are you doing here?"

She dug deep, working overtime to keep her voice casual, natural. "Landon offered me a ride home, but we realized it was getting late, so we came here first so he could shower. You guys are dropping me off at the pub on the way to the game."

Finn stepped across the threshold, glancing around the room.

She nearly winced when she spotted Landon's shorts and T-shirt from the game, discarded on the floor near the couch.

Finn spotted them as well.

She wasn't sure what she expected...but it wasn't her brother's tired sigh.

"What are you doing, Sun?"

She frowned. "What do you mean?"

"You know what I mean. You and Landon." He gestured toward the couch. "What is this?"

"We're just pretending to—"

"Don't," he interjected. "Don't tell me it's all just a game. Please."

She was about to do just that when he reached up and ran his knuckles over her cheek, near her lips.

"You have a bit of beard burn there."

Her fingers flew up to touch it. "I—" She blew out a frustrated breath. "I don't know what this is," she confessed, feeling a ridiculous amount of relief at having finally said those words aloud. Typically, she didn't have a thought she didn't share, either with her brother or Landon or her cousins.

This thing with Landon had thrown her for a loop. So much so, the words had gotten trapped inside with her jumbled-up feelings.

"Yeah. That's what I thought." There was no rebuke in Finn's tone. In fact, it was the opposite. He gave her a sympathetic smile that comforted her. Her big brother was here, and even if he didn't know how to make things right, he'd help her until she found her way.

"You're not mad at me?"

He snorted out a hard breath. "No."

"Why not?"

"Because you're not acting out of character. Let's face it. You never walk the straight and narrow. The wind blew you this direction and you went with it. Classic Sunnie."

As far as helpful, Finn's comments fell way short. Until she considered them more closely. Then she brightened up.

"You're right. It's not me who's acting strangely. It's Landon."

Finn shook his head. "No. He's not acting out of character either."

Sunnie was lost again. "I don't understand."

"Things have changed between you and Landon. Ever since that kiss. No, those kisses—the one at the party, and the one the night of the mugging. Landon sees that...but I don't think you do. And that's the problem. You're looking at this through the same Sunnie-colored glasses as always."

"Sunnie-colored glasses?" she asked with a grin.

One that vanished when he said, "I thought you'd take that description better than 'blinders.'"

"Finn—" she started, but before she could take her brother to task, Landon's voice drifted down the hallway.

"Just need a couple more minutes," he yelled from the direction of his bedroom. "Sorry I'm running so late, Finn."

"Promise me something, Sun?"

She didn't want to. Not because there wasn't anything she wouldn't do for her brother, but because she knew whatever he was going to ask for would be difficult for her to promise. "What?"

"Be careful."

She nodded without hesitation, his request surprisingly simple.

Or so she thought.

Until he added, "With his heart…and with yours."

## 13

Landon dropped Finn off after the Orioles game around ten. Then he went down to the pub, sat at the end of the bar and talked to Padraig until closing time.

If her cousin thought it was weird he was drinking alone, Padraig said nothing. Until last call.

"Going upstairs or going home?" Padraig asked.

That was the very question he'd been asking himself for the past few hours.

Landon shrugged. "I don't know."

"Sure you do. Just depends on which voice you listen to."

"Voice?" Landon asked.

"The one that's telling you it's smarter to go home or the one that's telling you you'd be a fool to leave."

"I'm in love with your cousin."

Padraig rubbed his chin. "Well, Finn's very fond of you too, but I'm not sure..." His joke fell off when he started to chuckle. "I know you are, Landon."

"You're not going to tell me I'm crazy? It's Sunnie we're talking about. She's reckless and wild and she goes through boyfriends the way some people go through underwear. She's practically been a sister to me my whole life."

Padraig winked at him. "Pretty sure that sister ship has sailed."

"She doesn't want a relationship. Doesn't want to settle down."

"Yet. She doesn't want to settle down *yet*."

Landon blew out a long breath. "So I should listen to the voice that says go home?"

Padraig shook his head. "I'm not going to tell you what to do because it's not my place. I'm only going to say this—life is too short for regrets, too short to not take a chance on your dreams."

"Mia..." Landon started, then stopped, hoping he hadn't upset Padraig by mentioning his late wife.

Padraig nodded. "Mia taught me that. She told me dream big. How big are your dreams, Landon?"

"I'm going upstairs."

Padraig chuckled. "Good decision."

Landon climbed the stairs, slowing when he reached the top and realized the television was still on. What would he say if Finn was still awake?

He continued on, only slightly relieved to find Colm sprawled out on the couch.

Colm sat up slowly when Landon appeared, his eyes narrowing briefly in confusion. Then he grinned.

"Which direction you headed?" Colm asked.

Like his twin brother, Colm saw everything Landon had been fighting like the devil to hide from Sunnie and Finn.

Landon pointed toward the hallway that led to Sunnie's room, the opposite direction from the staircase that would take him up to the extra bed in Finn's room.

Colm stood up and slapped him on the shoulder encouragingly. "Yeah. That's what I thought. Good luck. And um, I think this is my cue to go to bed. Don't want to run the risk of hearing anything you might do to my impressionable, sweet little cousin."

Landon chuckled. "Surprised you managed to say that whole thing without laughing."

"I'm a lawyer, used to spouting all kinds of bullshit. Just the same, if you do anything to hurt—"

"Colm. It's me."

That seemed to be all the reassurance Colm needed as he headed to the stairs, his room next door to Finn's on the third floor.

Landon walked to Sunnie's room, the door ajar. There was enough moonlight streaming into the room to allow him to see her. She'd already kicked the covers off and appeared to be wearing the same T-shirt/boxers deal she had on the morning he woke her for the interview.

He closed the door and locked it. Walking across the room, he pulled off his shirt, kicked off his shoes and socks and unfastened his jeans.

"Scoot over, Sunshine."

Landon sat on the edge of her bed. She barely stirred.

"Sunnie," he whispered, gently pushing her toward the center of the mattress.

She rolled with his soft shove, slowly coming awake and muttering something incomprehensible before pulling the pillow under her head and settling down again.

He chuckled softly as he shucked off his jeans and boxers.

"Sunnie," he said again, crawling in next to her.

She stirred once more, turning toward the sound of his voice.

"Landon?" she whispered.

"Yeah."

She shuffled, her head lifting from the pillow as if she didn't trust her hearing.

"What are you doing here? Wait. Are you naked?"

He grinned. "We're going to finish what we started earlier."

He recognized her hesitance, and he hated it.

"I..." She paused. "We need to be careful."

Nothing she could have said sounded less like Sunnie than

that. Landon had been waiting for a lecture from Finn throughout the entire baseball game tonight. It never came, so he realized he'd given it to Sunnie during Landon's shower.

"We're going to be careful, Sunshine," he assured her.

She obviously thought he misunderstood. "No, not that. I'm still on the pill. I mean—"

"I know exactly what you mean."

"You do?"

"I do." He pulled her toward him, kissing her, relieved when she returned his embrace, her lips going soft beneath him.

There wasn't a shy bone in Sunnie's body, so she lost no time taking advantage of his nudity. She ran her fingers over his bare chest, breaking off the kiss so she could look at him. He let her go, fully intending to take the same visual tour when he got her out of her pajamas.

"I've seen you without a shirt a million times. Why do I suddenly feel so..."

Landon forced himself to wait, to see what word she would use.

"God, I'm excited, nervous, and turned on all at the same time," she listed in one rushed breath.

"It's different this time."

Her gaze lifted to his. "Yeah. It is." Her hand drifted lower, gripping his cock as she had earlier today. "I haven't had sex in over a year."

He could tell from the slight wince that followed that statement she hadn't meant to blurt that out.

Landon smiled, giving her a soft, quick kiss. "Me either."

"You're, um...well, at the risk of giving you an inflated head... kind of big."

He laughed. "I'm not freaking John Holmes, Sunnie. It's going to be fine. Promise."

She rolled her eyes. "I know that. I'm just saying..."

"What?" he prompted, wondering what was worrying her.

"At April Fools, you told me what you like in bed, and I'm all in on...most of it."

He recalled what he said, and he knew exactly what part was freaking her out. "Jesus, Sunnie. I'm not doing all of that to you tonight. And I'm not doing anything you don't want or aren't comfortable with."

She nipped her lower lip, the gesture completely adorable, and for a second, she actually did fit Colm's description of impressionable and sweet. It passed quickly when she said, "While I wouldn't mind losing my anal cherry, I'm sure as hell not starting with this." She squeezed his dick firmly.

Landon laughed so hard, he fell to his back, her hand slipping off him. "Oh my God, Sunshine."

"What's so funny?" she asked, though her smile told him she wasn't offended by his humor.

"Anal cherry?"

"Well, it's not like I'm a virgin any other way. You should know that. After all, you were the first one I told when—"

"I know exactly when you lost your virginity," he said, cutting her off.

She'd lost it to Jacob Payne after the Homecoming football game her junior year. Sunnie had only gone out with him for two months and the decision to have sex had been based more on her determination to get rid of her pesky virginity than on true love. She'd missed her curfew, and knew her dad would question her about it, so she had called Landon and asked him to pick her up from Jacob's house, figuring Aaron would be more forgiving if she told him she'd been with Landon at the same party, and just lost track of time.

All that had happened was Aaron had read both of them the riot act, and Finn hadn't spoken to him the entire next day, pissed off Landon had gone to a party without him. The silent treatment for the party ended when Sunnie told Finn the truth and insisted he lay off Landon.

Of course, at that point, the silent treatment lasted even

longer. Finn was pissed as shit that Landon hadn't told him about Sunnie losing her virginity.

Landon reached out, tucking his arm around her. Sunnie laid her head on his chest, the two of them quiet for a moment.

"You know everything about me," she said after a few minutes. Landon couldn't quite read her tone.

"I don't think you can ever know everything about someone else. But it's safe to say I know a lot."

"You know a lot," she said, adopting his clarification. "And you still want to do this?"

"Of course I do."

She lifted her head, narrowing her eyes. "You think I'm a pain in the ass."

He twisted toward her. "I haven't thought that in years."

Sunnie kissed him, her tongue touching his. They remained that way for a long time, their lips connected as they shared the same air.

He moved it to the next level, helping her sit up so he could pull her T-shirt off. He'd had his lips on her breasts earlier today, in the locker room, but this was the first time she'd been completely topless, his view unobscured by a shirt or her bra.

Like her, he took some time to enjoy it. To touch her and look his fill.

"Lay down, so I can take these boxers off you."

She did as directed, lifting her hips as he gripped the elastic and pulled the last piece of clothing from her.

Sunnie squeezed her legs together briefly before parting them, so he could run his fingers over her slit.

She was wet and hot, just like she'd been this afternoon on his couch. He'd barely managed to stay at that goddamn baseball game, each inning lasting an eternity.

"Sunnie, I want to go slow, want to make this—"

"Shhh. If you've learned anything in the past couple weeks, it's that I go off like a bottle rocket every time you touch me. This won't take me long either."

He moved over her, her legs parting to welcome him between them. Once again, he let her guide him to her opening, and he pressed just the head inside. Then he paused.

"What are you waiting for?" she asked, when he made no move to go deeper.

"Finn."

She laughed—and that was when he thrust in, her giggles morphing to moans.

"Oh my God," she breathed.

He agreed. Nothing on earth could have prepared him for how good this felt.

He dropped to hold his weight on his elbows, kissing her as he slid in and out. He started slowly, giving her a chance to catch her breath, to adjust to him.

Soon, that wasn't enough.

He moved from his elbows to his hands, braced his knees and started moving harder, deeper.

Sunnie's grip on his shoulders tightened, her fingers digging in to his muscles there. Her hips moved in time, thrusting up as he pushed in.

After just a dozen rough strokes, she came.

Landon kept moving. Stopping would kill him. He had no doubt.

"Landon," she cried when he withdrew.

"Turn over," he said, helping her to her hands and knees. She groaned when he pushed back in from behind.

"*Fuck*," she said loudly. "Yes!"

He was glad Colm had gone to bed and vaguely wondered what the hell Yvonne was hearing. Her room was just next door.

He gripped her waist, thrusting roughly, Sunnie matching him.

"Hair," she gasped. "Do that thing—"

He didn't need to be asked twice...or once even.

Landon grasped a handful of her hair, pulling it.

Her pussy clenched in response. She was fucking perfect.

He lifted his hand, slapping one bare ass cheek, the other hand still buried in her hair. Sunnie exploded again, trembling violently as she came once more.

This time, he was a goner.

Landon jerked once, twice more, his balls constricting as he came.

"Holy fuck. Sunshine... Jesus!"

Neither of them moved immediately, locked together as they fought their way back to the surface.

Sunnie shivered as Landon withdrew, falling to the mattress next to her.

The room was quiet as both of them fought to catch their breath. Sunnie had reached out and found his hand. He held hers, squeezing it, as he tried to find the words.

Ever since that kiss at April Fools, Sunnie had consumed his thoughts and his fantasies.

She'd just blown every dirty daydream he'd had of her out of the water.

And while he'd been in love before, even thought he'd found "the one" in Audrey, he knew now those feelings had been lukewarm in comparison. If he'd married Audrey, he probably would have been happy, in an easy, comfortable way, but he would have missed out on spending the rest of his life with his soul mate.

Sunnie had been made for him.

Now he just had to convince *her*. She wouldn't go down easily. Certainly not without a fight.

At some point, her brain was going to kick in, going to tell her what they just did was a mistake. Which meant Landon needed to be ready.

Or maybe he could just keep her in this post-orgasm fog for the next fifty or so years.

He released her hand and turned toward her nightstand. Switching on the light, he opened the drawer.

Sunnie propped herself up on her elbow. "What do you think you're doing?"

"Looking for your vibrators."

Her face was priceless, the perfect blend of curiosity and horror. "Why?"

Landon didn't answer her. He didn't need to. He'd hit pay dirt. "Got it."

Pulling the vibrator out of the drawer, he was surprised to discover only that one toy.

"That's it?" he asked.

Sunnie flushed slightly.

"Are you blushing?"

She narrowed her eyes. "No," she protested hotly, her face growing even redder. Landon had never seen her look even remotely embarrassed, so his interest was piqued.

"Where are the rest of the toys, Sunnie?"

She pointed down. "Under the bed. They don't all...um...fit in the drawer."

Landon got out of bed, despite her grip on his arm as she attempted to keep him from exploring further.

"Wait!"

He reached beneath the bed and found a handle. Tugging the box out, he whistled at the size of it.

Then his eyes widened as he took off the lid. "Sweet Jesus," he murmured.

Sunnie's toy box rivaled the stockroom of Adam and Eve.

"What the hell, babe?" He lifted several items that were still in packages, including nipple clamps, handcuffs, a silk blindfold, and three different butt plugs.

"I had a coupon."

He shook his head. "Try again. Why isn't any of this opened?"

"It's new...ish."

"How new?" he asked, though he had a suspicion. He prayed it was correct.

She shrugged, but he merely stared her down, waiting.

"I got it a few months ago."

"Before or after April Fools."

Sunnie rolled her eyes, but the pink in her cheeks returned and his question was answered.

"You liked hearing what I enjoy in bed, didn't you? Turned you on."

She grabbed the butt plug and nipple clamps out of his hands and tossed them back in the box. "Put it away."

He shook his head, reaching for the cuffs and the blindfold. "We'll start slow."

She eyed the toys as he took them out of their packages.

"Why is the vibrator in the drawer and not the box?"

She lifted one shoulder casually. "It's my favorite."

"Perfect."

He tossed the lid back on the box and toed it under the bed once more before sitting next to her.

"Landon, I don't think—"

"If you want to say no, Sunnie, say it and these go away. But you and I both know you bought them because you were curious." He spun the cuffs around on one finger. They were velvet-lined, made for sexual bondage. If she really got into being restrained, he'd love to use the real thing on her. Roleplay with Sunnie would be a lot of fun.

Sunnie considered his offer, her flush fading as she crawled toward him. His dick went hard as she moved slowly, sensually across the bed.

"You know how to use those, Officer Riggs?"

Oh fuck.

It was on.

"Are you going to come peacefully, or are you planning to resist arrest?"

"I never come peacefully. I'm pretty sure you just heard exactly how loud I come."

"Sunnie," Landon said, his voice suddenly husky with need.

"Hmmm?" As she hummed, she reached out, intent on grasping his cock in her hand.

He took a step away. If she touched him, this ended before it began. He'd have her flat on her back and he'd be inside her within seconds, fucking her like his life depended on it.

This was one game he intended to play all the way out.

"You have the right to remain silent, Ms. Young," he started, his deep cop voice capturing her attention.

"Can't we work something out, Officer Riggs? Make some other sort of arrangement so I don't have to go to jail?"

"Are you attempting to bribe me?" he asked, feigning offense.

Sunnie ran her fingers along his chest. "I don't have any money, but..."

"But," he prompted.

"Maybe there's something else I can give you."

"I'd be very careful, Ms. Young. I'm an honest cop, and anything you say now can and will be used against you."

He purposely didn't finish his line.

"In a court of law?" she added.

Landon shook his head. "In my bed."

Before she could reply to that, he turned her away from him, draping her facedown on the bed. She struggled slightly, her resistance a token effort at best as she kept up the pretense.

"Please, Officer," she said breathlessly.

Once her hands were secured behind her back, he drew the blindfold on over her eyes. Sunnie shook her head as he tried to tie it, and this time her struggle felt genuine. She wouldn't like the loss of her vision—it would strip away some of the control she thought she had.

She was about to find out how little of that she actually possessed.

"If it's too much for you, Sunshine...if you get scared, just say 'cheerleader' and I'll stop."

She snickered. "You're so obsessed with me in that uniform."

He followed that taunt with a slap to her ass. A hard one.

Sunnie jerked, in surprise and perhaps even a bit of pain.

"Ow."

"What do you say to make me stop?" he prompted.

"Cheerleader," she breathed. "But, Landon—"

He smacked her again. "Officer Riggs," he corrected.

She shivered slightly. "Officer Riggs?"

"Yes."

"I won't say that word. I don't want to stop."

Just when he thought his dick couldn't get any harder.

Landon pressed her legs apart and sank three fingers in deep. She was slick with arousal and his come, and her inner muscles quivered, still sensitive from the orgasms she'd already had.

When she started moving in time with his thrusting fingers, he withdrew them.

"Don't stop," she demanded, her request earning her another slap to her ass.

"I don't think you understand how serious your crimes were, Ms. Young," he said, reminding her they were still playing their roles. Landon knelt behind her.

Sunnie tilted her head, forced to guess what he was doing, blinded by the silk over her eyes. She appeared to be listening for clues.

He grinned, wondering what she'd make of what she heard next.

Landon pulled the box back out. He'd shoved it away, wanting her to relax, to think the only toys he intended to play with were the cuffs and blindfold.

"What are you—" she started.

He cut her off with a hard spank. "Quiet."

Sunnie pressed her lips together tightly, and he could tell she was struggling to remain in character. She was too inquisitive, too demanding.

Submission would never come natural to her.

Of course, that didn't mean she wouldn't enjoy it. Even now, the inside of her thighs shone with her arousal. She was very, very wet. And ready.

He tugged out the smallest of the butt plugs and a tube of

lubrication. Landon opened the packages, watching her face, turned toward him as she still tried to figure out what he was doing. There was no question she was dying to ask. Remarkably, she was a quick study, and she kept her mouth shut.

Picking up her vibrator, he slowly slid it into her pussy, enjoying her soft moan of relief. That would be short-lived, but he let her think she knew what was going on. The thing was a rabbit, so once it was fully lodged, he lined up the clit tickler part, rubbing her clit with his fingers as she released a long, hard shudder.

She whispered "God" breathlessly, but he let her have that one word, not spanking her for breaking her silence.

Once the vibrator was in place, he turned it on low, enjoying her slight jerk and deep moan of desire.

Then he stood up. "Stay there."

Her hands were cuffed behind her back, the vibrator in her pussy, but she wasn't restrained to the bed. If she wanted to stand up, she could.

His request caught her off guard.

"Wait. What?"

He replied to her question with four smacks to her ass and upper thighs, each one rocking the vibrator deeper, her hips thrusting in need of more friction.

Landon bent over her, his chest pressed firmly to her back as he whispered in her ear.

"I don't repeat myself, Ms. Young, but since this is your first arrest, I'll say it again. Stay here. Don't move. I'll know if you do—and trust me, while you might like being spanked, I don't think you'll enjoy the feel of my belt on your ass quite as much."

"Oh God. Why is this so fucking hot?" Sunnie completely fell out of character, and it took everything Landon had not to laugh.

Tomorrow, he was making a list of every roleplay he'd ever fantasized about. He and Sunnie were doing them all.

Landon nipped at her earlobe, letting that serve as his warning. "Don't move."

He pushed himself up, grabbing the butt plug and walking to the door. Sadly, she and Yvonne shared the bathroom at the end of the hall. He briefly considered throwing on his boxers, but that thin layer of cotton wasn't going to hide the erection that wasn't going anywhere until it was buried balls deep in Sunnie.

Opening the door, he glanced down the hall, sent up a silent prayer that he didn't run into anyone—thus gaining the nickname Naked Landon—and he headed out, closing the bedroom door behind him to protect Sunnie's modesty.

The gods were smiling on him. The apartment was silent, everyone sound asleep.

He washed the butt plug, then tiptoed back to the room. He opened the door stealthily, curious to see if Sunnie had obeyed his orders.

She was wiggling like a worm on a hook, her toes pressed to the floor, her hips in the air as she swayed, trying to steal whatever relief she could.

He'd purposely left the vibrator on low, knowing it wouldn't be enough to push her over, just enough to keep her motor revving, her body reaching for more.

Landon shut the door with a soft snick and Sunnie froze in place, clearly caught in the act.

He crossed the room and spanked her twice. "What part of 'don't move' were you struggling with?"

She opened her mouth, clearly ready to offer some smart-ass reply, but he spanked her again.

"Quiet."

Time to up the ante. Show her exactly what she was in for with him. Too many years of listening to her call him Boy Scout were coming to the forefront. Landon grinned. Sunnie was about to meet *his* bad boy.

Uncapping the lubrication, he pressed the tip to her anus and squeezed.

She shrieked with surprise when the gel slid in. "Wait!" she cried out.

Landon ran the tip of his finger over her anus. "That's not the word that's going to make me stop," he said, reminding her that she had a safe word if she wanted this to end. He prayed to God she didn't use it.

Sunnie stilled, but didn't speak. He could practically see the wheels spinning in her brain.

He didn't give her time to think too hard about it. Landon pressed in, just to the first knuckle.

Sunnie, for all her wiggling earlier, had gone completely still.

He didn't mistake that for disinterest. He had her attention —all of it. She wasn't going to stop him. He was certain of it.

Landon pressed in farther, until one finger was completely lodged in her ass.

He considered asking her how it felt, if she wanted to go on. That's what Landon would do. But they were playing different parts right now, and he knew Sunnie was enjoying that as much as he was.

"It takes a lot of work to subdue you," he murmured.

Sunnie didn't respond, and he realized she seemed lost in the moment. It was beautiful.

He took his time, thrusting just one finger into her ass, over and over, slowly, until she was relaxed enough that he decided to add a second, then finally a third.

The vibrator was still on low, still pulsing in her pussy.

Landon wasn't sure how long he'd been playing with her, stretching her. He'd been pushing her toward her orgasm by inches. Last time, they'd both been too ready, too anxious to race to the finish line.

This time, they were savoring each and every moment, every sensation.

She shuddered roughly when he pulled his fingers out of her ass, replacing it with the butt plug and more lube.

"Oh my God," she whispered.

Landon freed her hands from the cuffs and pulled the blindfold from her eyes.

Sunnie blinked a few times, adjusting to the sudden light. He hadn't turned off the nightstand lamp, hadn't wanted to miss watching her responses to everything he did to her.

"Roll over, Sunnie," he said.

She smiled, aware that the roleplay was over.

He gripped the end of the vibrator, pulling it out as her back arched.

"I need…"

"I know," he whispered.

He lifted her on the bed, positioning her in the middle of the mattress. The plug was still in her ass, adding a delicious tightness they both felt as he pushed his cock inside her.

Once there, he held the position, kissing her for several minutes.

"You're so beautiful," he murmured, his compliment producing a sweet smile.

Her hands rested on his shoulders, but after he spoke, she drew one palm to his cheek, cupping it, looking at him like he hung the moon.

For her, he would do anything.

He took her slowly, making love to her.

Landon knew the difference between that and fucking. He wondered if Sunnie felt it as well.

Her inner muscles clenched and Landon groaned. He wasn't going to be able to hold back.

She was too tight, too wet…too perfect.

He kissed her until she turned her head, gasping for breath, her eyes closing as her orgasm crashed over her.

She took Landon with her, and he came, filling her, taking her lips again.

They kissed the entire time and long after, him caging her beneath him, his dick going soft inside her.

Finally, he pushed to the side, drawing her toward him.

She rested her head on his chest, and he thought perhaps she'd drifted to sleep.

"I need to take that plug out," he whispered.

Sunnie lifted her head then reached back, taking care of it herself. He heard it thump once as she dropped it to the floor. She returned to her previous position without a word.

Sunnie was never quiet. But it was more than her lack of talking that took his breath away at the moment. It was the utter peace on her face.

She had a faraway look in her eyes that told him, for this moment, she was exactly where she wanted to be. That she didn't have a single regret.

He prayed that contentment lasted until morning.

No. He hoped it lasted forever.

## ❧ 14 ❧

Sunnie stood by the window in her scrubs, looking down at the street outside the pub. Her shift at the hospital started in an hour.

It was a quiet Sunday morning. No one out and about except a handful of joggers and people heading to church.

No reporters. No women.

It occurred to her the crowds following them had vanished at least a few days ago. And yet, they'd carried on with his plan, acting like a couple.

Her stomach ached and her heart was racing, but she couldn't figure out why.

Last night had been...

God...it had been everything.

Landon had shown up in her bedroom and even though she knew it was a mistake, she'd let him stay, let him in. Her body, her mind, her—

She shoved the last word away.

Not her heart. Definitely not her heart.

Time to take a big step back and approach this unfamiliar feeling with reasoning.

She'd had sex with Landon, her brother's best friend.

*Her* best friend.

She blew out a long, frustrated, slightly shaky breath. How were they supposed to find their way back to any sort of normal after everything they'd done last night?

He'd tied her up, spanked her, put a butt plug in her ass and given her so many orgasms, she'd lost count.

It had been amazing. Wonderful. Un-fucking-believable.

So why was she so scared?

Because he wanted more. She knew that. The same way he knew she didn't.

Sunnie didn't have a clue how to be anyone's girlfriend. There was no way she wouldn't fuck this up, and when she did...

She'd lose him.

Forever.

Her thoughts were flying around so fast and furious, she felt dizzy. Her stomach lurched and for a second, she thought she might be sick.

"Sunnie," Landon called to her from the bed.

She didn't glance his direction. Didn't dare face him after... everything they'd done.

"Scrubs?" he asked. She was grateful he couldn't see the panic on her face.

"I have to be at work in an hour." So far, so good. Her voice sounded relatively normal.

"Damn. I didn't realize. I've got the day off. I was hoping we could spend it in bed."

Her chest went tight. Maybe she was having a heart attack. Heart disease was the number one killer in women. She wiggled her left arm, checking for numbness.

Nope. Not a heart attack.

"Sorry. No can do," she said, going for some sort of lightness. It had sounded strained to her, but Landon appeared to buy it.

"When is your lunch break? I can meet you in the hospital cafeteria. Or a storage closet," he teased. "I'm up for a hot date with my sexy nurse."

His words tweaked her overwrought nerves. Him and his fucking dates. And kisses. They were what had landed them in this mess. He'd played loose and free with their friendship and now she was a nervous wreck.

"Sunnie?" he said, when she didn't respond.

"Is it all still pretend, Landon?" This time, she failed to school her tone.

He didn't respond. Part of her wanted to turn, to face him, to read the truth on his face. She was too afraid to do that. Afraid he'd see too much in her face as well.

The room was silent. No doubt he was considering his answer, seeking the safest path. That thought annoyed her.

"Is it still pretend?" she repeated.

"Look at me, Sunshine."

The sound of his nickname for her triggered something unexpected, something almost painful.

She shook her head. "No."

"Dammit, Sunnie. Look at me."

Stealing herself, she turned toward him, fighting to calm her racing heart, her shaking hands.

Landon gave her a sweet smile. "It was never pretend. Not for me."

She knew that. She'd always known it, but fear was setting in deep and she was spiraling out of control. "You lied. You lied about everything. About the reason for pretending to date me."

Landon sat up, his bare legs hanging over the edge of the bed. "Lie feels like a strong word."

"You lied to me instead of manning up and asking me out." There was a tinge of anger in her voice that she hated.

He crossed his arms, drawing her attention to his muscular biceps, his six-pack abs. She closed her eyes.

*Don't look at the pretty man.*

"What would you have said if I'd asked you out for a date?" he asked.

She forced herself to look at him as she told him the truth. "I would have said no."

"Why?"

"*Why?*"

Landon started to stand, but she shook her head, waved for him to stay where he was. Right now, the sheet covered him from the waist down. If he stood up, revealed that he was still naked, she'd remember everything they'd done…and how much she wanted to do it again.

He relented, remaining where he was. "Why would you have said no?"

Landon never let her get away with just saying something vague. He always called her on it, expected her to dig deeper, to say more.

She sucked at that.

Why would she have said no?

This time she actually had the answer. Sunnie started throwing up fingers as she ticked off everything on her list, fighting to bring some semblance of reason back to this. "Because we're complete opposites, a total mismatch. Because we're at two different places in our lives. I don't want a relationship. You do. Because you're practically my freaking brother. You're Finn's best friend. And you work for my dad."

"Is that it?"

She threw her hands up, frustrated and…terrified. "How many more things do I need?"

"Aren't you missing the big one?"

Sunnie fell silent, uncertain what he meant.

Landon stood up, the sheet falling away as he crossed the room toward her. Her gaze dropped to his erection. Despite her obvious anger toward him, he was hard as a rock.

"No," she said hastily. "That's not happening again."

She lifted her hands, putting them on his chest to hold him back when he got too close.

"Tell me the *real* reason you're fighting with me, Sunnie."

"I told you."

"None of that is what's holding you back."

She hated the assurance in his voice. God, it was almost smug. And why not? He knew her. He knew freaking everything about her. Even so, she longed to knock him down a peg. To prove that in this argument, she was right and he was wrong.

"Okay, Mr. Arrogant. Hit me with it. Tell me why you think I'm mad."

"You're afraid of falling in love, Sunnie. And that's *exactly* what's happened."

She snorted, dismissing his assertion, even as she feared he might be right. She swallowed heavily, refusing to give him the point. "Get over yourself, Landon. It was only one night."

And the most amazing sex on the planet.

He grinned. Stood there in the face of her panic, his dick rock-hard, and gave her the sweetest, most pure Landon grin in his arsenal.

"You're insane," she struck out. "This isn't love. It's lust."

"Nope. It's love."

"You're wrong. And I'm not doing this."

He tilted his head. "Doing what, Sunshine?"

"Stop calling me that!" Her words came out much louder than she'd intended. She was practically shouting at him. "My name is Sunday. And..." She sucked in a deep, pained breath. It made a noise, one that made her feel weak.

Landon's eyes softened, his smile fading, replaced by a concerned look that made her feel worse than weak. It made her feel stupid, vulnerable.

"And I'm going to be late to work. I have to leave."

"Sunnie. Please. Wait."

She shook her head. She needed to get away from him, needed air, needed to cry her fucking eyes out.

In love?

There's no way that's what this feeling was.

Was there?

She rushed out, deftly dodging Landon as he reached out, attempted to grab her, hold her. She had the advantage because she was fully dressed, shoes and all.

She darted through the living room, grabbing her purse and keys, even as she heard Landon calling out her name. He was no doubt struggling to pull on his jeans.

"Sunnie?" Finn was coming down the stairs.

She held up her hand and he stopped mid-step. "Not one word, Finn. I can't...deal with you right now."

"What are you talk..." His words faded away as she continued down the stairs.

Sunnie took a deep breath when she reached the foot of the stairs, then tried to slow her pace as she walked into the pub. Shit, she was still moving too fast, but there was only forty feet between her and the exit. If she could make it, she'd hide at work until...

Maybe she could just live at work indefinitely. It had already been a hell of a morning, and she'd only been awake an hour. There were still too many family members to escape, and she wasn't sure she could handle a bunch of questions about Landon right now.

"Hey, Sunnie," Yvonne called out from Sunday's Side.

"Can't talk," Sunnie said, barely glancing back. "Late to work."

She was grateful her cousin didn't persist. Once she hit the sidewalk, Sunnie practically ran to her car, afraid Landon would catch up to her.

If he did...she didn't know how she'd react. Her panic was growing with each step. She shouldn't have run out like that, but goddammit...what else could she do?

*Stay here.*

*Act like an adult.*

She shoved those insane thoughts away as she climbed into her car, started it, and pulled onto the street.

By the time she made it to the hospital, she realized her

hands were shaking. And she was crying.

LANDON DIDN'T BOTHER TO THROW ON MORE THAN HIS JEANS and tennis shoes before he darted out into the living room.

Finn stood at the head of the stairs that led down to the pub, looking perplexed until he turned and saw Landon there —shirtless.

"Shit," Finn muttered.

"You can punch me later," Landon said. "Right now..." He gestured toward the stairs.

"She's long gone, man. And believe me, chasing her would be your worst move."

There wasn't much Finn could have said that would've made him give up his pursuit of Sunnie at the moment...except that.

"Why?"

"Because she's in the middle of freaking out. Sunnie is completely unreasonable in that frame of mind, and you know it. Give her some time to land and *then* chase after her."

Landon sighed. Finn was right. And while his head said giving her space was a good idea, he wasn't feeling particularly rational at the moment.

"So..." Finn started, walking over to the couch and sitting down. "When did you come back?"

Landon followed him, dropping into the recliner. It was time he and Finn talked. "I never left. Went down to the pub until closing time. Then came back up here."

Finn considered that. "Padraig try to stop you, or did he suggest it?"

Landon shrugged. "He gave me some good advice that encouraged me. Colm was here on the couch when I showed up."

Finn nodded. "He's a night owl whenever he's got a big case on his mind. Given your shirtless state, I can see there are no bruises. I'm assuming *he* didn't try to stop you either."

Landon shook his head. "Wished me luck."

Finn leaned forward, resting his elbows on his knees. "You got it bad, huh?"

"Yeah."

"Let me guess. You woke up and started talking about love and commitment and all that shit. You should have known better, man."

"Actually, she was freaking out before I woke up. I think last night—"

Finn raised his hand to cut him off. "I don't want to know one damn thing about last night. You give me too many details and I'll have to beat the shit out of you on principle. I know way too much about your bedroom games."

Landon grinned. Finn knew about them because it was one way in which they were actually very similar. Like Landon, Finn enjoyed bondage and rough play and control.

"Give me some credit. I'm not going to tell you what we did...or how many times." He wiggled his eyebrows, getting a kick out of Finn's sudden scowl. Once the shock of Landon and Sunnie being together as a couple wore off, Landon was going to have a hell of a lot of fun at Finn's expense, the perfect payback for years of teasing and practical jokes.

"Probably going to need therapy to get through this," Finn joked. "Wonder if Uncle Chad has any room on his schedule this week. Not sure I could sit on Aunt Lauren's couch and talk about," he pointed to Landon's shirtless chest again, "this."

Landon tried to smile, but he couldn't get the image of Sunnie standing by the window out of his mind. He knew her standard operating procedure whenever a guy got too close, but he'd foolishly thought it would be different with him. For one thing, he wasn't a fucking tool. And what they'd done, the way it had been between them... God, Landon had never experienced anything like that.

"I'm in over my goddamned head here, bro," Landon confessed. "She's got my heart in her teeth."

"I warned you the other week that—"

"You're not seriously going to hit me with 'I told you so,' are you?"

"Of course I'm not. Or," Finn grinned, "I'm not going to say *just* that. It's enough that you and I both know I did tell you this would happen. And you didn't listen. Not that I thought you would. So get your game plan together. Taking off after her would have just added more steam to the pressure cooker and she would have blown. You have to give her a chance to let what happened sink in. My sister's not stupid. She's stubborn as hell, but she'll reason this out soon enough, and when she does, she'll figure out what you already know."

"What's that?"

"That you're perfect for each other."

Landon didn't realize how much Finn's support meant to him until that second. "You really believe that?"

"There's not one single guy on this planet I'd want with my sister more than you."

"So...what's my next move?"

"Nothing. The next move is hers."

Landon shook his head. "No. She'll never—"

"Dammit, man. If you push her on this, she'll only dig in her heels harder. I'm going downstairs for breakfast. Want to come with me?"

Landon shrugged, food was the last thing he wanted. Then he nodded. He didn't have anything else to do, and the idea of going home alone and stewing all day wasn't appealing. Truth was, he didn't see himself going home until he saw Sunnie again, which would be hours from now. "Yeah. Okay. Day drink at the pub in front of the games?"

Finn was always in for that. "Hell yeah."

"Just let me," Landon grinned as he looked down, making sure to point out a red mark above his nipple, a souvenir left behind by Sunnie, "get dressed."

Finn sighed. "Shit. I'm probably still gonna have to kick your ass."

Landon chuckled, then walked back to Sunnie's room. His cell phone was on the nightstand. Glancing over his shoulder, he picked it up and failed to follow Finn's advice.

He texted Sunnie.

*Need to talk.*

A full minute passed before her reply came back, and he realized his best friend had been right.

*Can't. Not yet.*

Landon wanted to push her, but instead he swallowed down the lump in his throat and took a steadying breath.

He wasn't finished fighting for Sunnie's heart.

Not by a long shot.

"**G**et in."

Sunnie recognized the voice, surprised when she looked over and saw her cousin Yvonne pulled up to the curb outside the hospital, passenger window rolled down to get her attention. She was coming off a ten-hour shift, her feet hurt, her eyes were scratchy from crying, and the idea of going home and possibly seeing Landon had her stomach in knots.

She'd hoped a day of hard work would shake out some of her confusion, but it hadn't touched it. Hell, she was in worse shape now, the initial panic turning to cold-blooded terror.

She was a hot mess.

"What are you doing here?" Sunnie asked.

Kelli, whom she hadn't noticed until that point, peeked her head over the back seat. "We're kidnapping you. Taking you out for margaritas. Get your ass in the car."

"What about *my* car?" she stupidly asked, even though she was already reaching for the door handle.

"I'll drive you back for it in the morning." Yvonne had clearly thought through this kidnapping.

She was quiet as Yvonne pulled out of the parking lot and onto the street. "Why the kidnapping?" she asked at last.

Yvonne glanced over and winked. "Because I saw you this morning, running out of the Collins Dorm like you were being chased by a serial killer. It was obvious you'd just pulled a Sunnie, especially considering the way Landon's been holding up the bar ever since. So, Kelli and I decided you needed an intervention. And *we* needed margaritas."

"Pulled a Sunnie?" she asked.

"AKA, dumped the dude and ran for the hills," Kelli chimed in from the back.

"It's Sunday night," Sunnie said to Kelli. "School night."

"And it's June," Kelli reminded her. "I'm one week into my summer vacay bender. Fucking free. And it feels great!"

Kelli was a kindergarten teacher and Padraig's best friend. She'd also been around as long as Landon, which meant—like him—she was practically family.

*Family.*

Sunnie's stomach clenched again, and she debated telling Yvonne to pull over in case she got sick.

Sunnie rubbed her eyes wearily. "Listen. I don't want you all to think I don't appreciate this, but—"

"Save it. This is happening." Yvonne turned on her blinker and pulled into the parking lot of their favorite Mexican restaurant. While the food was just okay, they made killer margaritas. "Come on."

Kelli and Yvonne both got out, leaving Sunnie no choice but to follow.

Once they'd claimed a booth, ordered chips and salsas, and three frozen margaritas, Yvonne lifted her hand and said, "Let's have it. What happened?"

Sunnie knew her cousin and Kelli. Knew she'd never leave this restaurant until she spilled her guts. But now that she was here, she realized talking about it with them was probably exactly what she needed. Her thoughts were a jumbled mess. "How far back do I need to go?"

Yvonne shot her a dirty look. "Given the dark circles under

my eyes, I think you can go ahead and assume I'm up to speed through three a.m. That's when I put the earplugs in."

Sunnie winced. "Sorry."

"Don't be. I couldn't hear what you were saying, but there was a fair amount of mattress squeaking and headboard banging. Gotta hand it to Landon—sounds like he's got stamina."

Sunnie laughed and the tightness in her chest eased a little. "It was amazing sex. You couldn't believe—"

"Whoa, whoa, whoa," Kelli said. "I'm going to need *a lot* more details. I missed the sound effects last night."

The waitress brought their drinks and Sunnie lifted hers, clinking it against Kelli and Yvonne's glasses. "Can I just say it was the best sex of my life?"

Kelli sighed. "Damn. Where can I sign up for some of that?"

"Of course it was," Yvonne said. "It's that old friends-to-lovers thing. It always survives the test of time."

Sunnie winced when Yvonne said the word lovers, prompting her cousin to roll her eyes.

"So if the sex was so great, what happened this morning to send you running?" Kelli asked.

Sunnie sighed. "I freaked out."

Kelli shook her head, as if disappointed in her, while Yvonne said, "Of course you did."

Sunnie had too much pride for her own good, so Yvonne's response put her on the defensive. "He lied to me, Vonnie. Said we were just going to," she finger-quoted, "'pretend date.' He wasn't pretending."

"Don't be that girl, Sun," Yvonne said.

"What girl?"

Yvonne looked at Kelli, who lifted a hand, gesturing for her to continue.

"The stupid one. You knew it wasn't pretend."

Sunnie swallowed heavily, not ready to admit that. "Finn will never accept this. Landon is his best friend. I'm his sister."

"Oh my God," Kelli said. "*That* girl is worse."

Sunnie leaned back, exasperated. "Which girl is that?"

"The one who uses other people as excuses for her own stupidity. Go back to just being thick." Kelli picked up her margarita and took a drink.

The weight that had been pressing down on her chest since she woke up this morning lifted a bit more, and Sunnie grinned, even as she said, "I hate both of you."

Kelli laughed and kept drinking.

Yvonne smiled, unoffended. "No, you don't. I'm your best friend/cousin. You're crazy about me."

Sunnie shrugged. "I think I've changed my mind about that. Might pick Caitlyn or Ailis for that role."

"They have each other."

"Fiona," Sunnie said.

"She lives too far away. Besides, she's got two gay best friends. She'll never have time for you."

Sunnie laughed, then the three of them fell silent for a few moments, eating chips, drinking margaritas, giving her a chance to let their words sink in.

Finally, she said the thing that had caused her stupid freak-out to begin with. "Landon thinks I'm in love with him."

"You are."

The more Yvonne kept pointing out the obvious, the more Sunnie wished she could rewind her morning freak-out. "Well, obviously I love him. I've always loved him. It's just..."

"You've never been *in* love, Sunnie. You've never really set yourself up for that emotion because your taste in men was pretty shallow. Pretty faces and big muscles." Kelli leaned closer and winked. "Not that I fault you for that. Some of those boys were very, very easy to look at."

Sunnie laughed again, figuring Kelli probably understood her the best. Like Sunnie, Kelli wasn't looking to settle down, and her track record with men wasn't much better.

Then Sunnie said, "Those guys were easy to be with. No expectations. No commitment. This is..."

"Hard," Yvonne finished for her.

Sunnie nodded, then spoke her real fear. "What if it doesn't work out, Vonnie? If I screw this up, or he figures out it was a mistake...it'll kill me. I hate feeling so scared."

Yvonne reached over the table and grasped her hand, squeezing it. "That's what I mean by hard. But you're not going to mess anything up. And no part of this is a mistake—*Landon* knows that. Love is one big-ass risk. But believe me, you and Landon are a pretty safe bet. I'd put all my money on you."

Kelli lifted her glass and toasted her. "Me too."

Sunnie smiled, still not completely convinced.

Yvonne recognized her doubtful expression. "You saw the video, Sun. You saw how Landon looked at you after that kiss. How can you doubt his feelings aren't completely genuine?"

Sunnie closed her eyes and sighed. "I only watched it once. And I wasn't looking at him. I was kind of looking at my hair. There was this one piece—" she continued, reaching up.

"One time?" Kelli interrupted in disbelief. "I've probably seen it *fifty* times."

"You watched it one time?" Yvonne repeated, equally shocked.

Sunnie nodded. "Yeah. You should know. You were there."

"That's the *only* time you saw the video? Jesus! No wonder you're acting like an idiot. The second we get home, you're going to go upstairs, alone, pull out your phone, turn off the stupid canned music in the background and watch the damn thing. Look at *Landon*. Screw your hair!"

"Pop Pop told me to do the same thing." Sunnie didn't point out that advice had come a few weeks earlier.

"And as always, Pop Pop was right. I can't believe you didn't listen to him."

"I was scared," Sunnie confessed. "I'm *still* scared."

"Which is why we're here," Yvonne said, lifting her margarita. "We're going to fortify you with a couple of these, then you can go home and watch the video."

"Then you can find Landon and tell him you love him," Kelli added.

"Just do me a favor?" Yvonne added.

"Anything," Sunnie said, grateful for her cousin and Kelli. They had made everything so much better.

"Sleep at his place tonight."

Sunnie laughed as she picked up a chip, dipping it into the salsa. Now that she had a plan, the appetite that had eluded her all day returned with a vengeance. "You got it."

"Another round?" Kelli suggested.

Sunnie nodded. "And fajitas. I'm starving."

$\maltese$  16  $\maltese$

Landon sat at the end of the bar with Miguel and Finn, watching the Orioles game. They'd been here all damn day. It was growing late, which meant that for the past two hours, he'd had one eye on the television and the other on the door.

He had spent the entire day trying to figure out what he'd say to Sunnie that might set her mind at ease, that wouldn't cause her to freak out again.

Sunnie had told him countless times she wasn't looking for a relationship, that she wanted to focus on her career. He respected that, but as far as he was concerned, she could have her career and him at the same damn time.

And that ridiculous list she'd rattled off this morning was full of nothing. Finn had already given his blessing, and Landon suspected—hoped—Aaron and Riley would do the same.

Which left the love part.

She'd never been in love, and he could understand why that might scare her. He'd seen honest-to-God panic in her eyes this morning and it had bothered him all day.

"Landon?"

Landon turned at the sound of her voice, thinking he'd misheard. There was no way...

Audrey stood behind him, smiling.

"Audrey?"

He stood up, giving her a hug, catching Finn's shocked expression as Miguel mouthed *The Audrey?* to Finn, who nodded just once. He and Miguel had been partnered up on the force a couple of months after Audrey left town, so the two of them had never met.

"I stopped by your place but you weren't there. I hoped I might find you here."

"Why didn't you call and tell me you were in town?" he asked.

"I wanted to surprise you."

She'd done that. And not in a great way. Two minutes ago, he'd been wishing Sunnie would hurry up and get home. Now he was hoping he could buy a few more minutes.

She smiled and said hello to Finn, and he introduced her to Miguel, the three of them exchanging pleasantries as Landon tried to figure out how he could politely tell her this wasn't a good time.

"I was wondering," Audrey said, turning back to him, "if I could speak to you alone for a moment or two?"

He wanted to say no, but he noticed her eyes were shiny and it looked like she might cry. Had something happened to someone in her family?

"Of course," he said, gesturing to the only empty booth left in the pub, in the back corner. Audrey sat first, grabbing the side that faced the doorway, which left Landon at a disadvantage. He now had his back to not only the front door, but the stairs that led to the Collins Dorm. Short of constantly turning around, he had no way to know when Sunnie arrived home.

Sighing, he sat as well, but before he could ask what was wrong, Darcy—who'd just started waiting tables at the pub a few months earlier—was standing there. She said hello to Audrey, asked if she wanted anything to drink, then shot Landon a not-so-subtle *what the hell* look.

Finn had filled his kid sister in on Sunnie and Landon's newfound relationship—skipping over the sex part, even though it was clear that was all Darcy was interested in hearing about—shortly after lunchtime.

Landon had carried his full pint over with him from the bar, so he waited...and just barely resisted muttering a curse when Audrey ordered a glass of wine and then asked to see a food menu. The last thing he wanted to do right now was have a drink and dinner with his ex-girlfriend. He and Audrey had parted on good terms, and while he wouldn't mind catching up with her someday—preferably with Sunnie there—tonight wasn't the night for that.

"How have you been?" she asked.

"Fine. And you?"

"I've been..." She paused, and he caught just a glimpse of the sadness he'd spotted earlier before she pasted on a smile and said, "Good. Busy with auditions."

"Any parts coming your way?"

She shook her head. "It's a very competitive atmosphere. Between waiting tables, taking acting classes, and auditions, I'm lucky if I get six hours of sleep every night."

"You knew it would take some time. I'm sure you're right there on the cusp of something big."

Audrey nodded, clearly not agreeing. "I'm thinking about moving back to Baltimore."

Landon wasn't sure how to respond to that. If she'd told him the same thing a year ago, he would have been thrilled, excited, ready to jump right back in where they'd left off. Mercifully, that hadn't happened, because he couldn't begin to imagine wanting that life over this one. Even with Sunnie still fighting her feelings for him.

"Audrey. It's only been a year or so. Are you sure you've given it—"

"I started dating someone right after I moved to New York."

Her abrupt right turn caught him off guard. "Okay."

"He was an actor too. We'd go to auditions together and around Thanksgiving, we moved in together."

Landon thought back to Thanksgiving. He'd eaten lunch with his mom and stepdad, then headed to the Collins Dorm later that night for a Tom-Hanks-giving marathon. He had still been nursing a broken heart, down in the dumps and missing Audrey. Sunnie and Finn knew, of course, and had come up with the movie marathon as a way of keeping him distracted.

Obviously, Audrey had rebounded a hell of a lot faster than he had.

"Why are you telling me this, Audrey?" he asked, wondering where this conversation was going and hoping she'd get to the point soon. He really wanted to return to the bar to keep an eye out for Sunnie.

"The first time he hit me was Christmas day."

Landon's stomach dropped. "What?"

Audrey forced a smile that didn't fool him, lifted one shoulder—feigning a casualness that didn't work, then said, "Not all guys are nice."

"Audrey." He reached across the table and grasped her hand as she swiped away a tear with the other. "I'm sorry."

Sunnie wasn't two steps in the pub when she was surrounded by Finn, Darcy and Miguel.

"What's up, guys?" she asked, trying to look around them for Landon, the task impossible, thanks to the wall they'd built.

"Not much. How are things with you?" Darcy asked, her voice way too cheery.

Sunnie instantly went on the alert.

Kelli had already moved around her, heading to the bar to talk to Padraig. Yvonne, also unimpeded, followed her.

Sunnie noticed when they both saw something and stopped mid-step.

That was when they came back and added two more bricks to the wall.

"What the fuck?" Sunnie insisted, trying to dodge them.

"Why don't we all move the party upstairs?" Yvonne suggested. "You can change out of your scrubs and we'll turn the intervention into a slumber party."

"Great idea," Kelli said.

Sunnie wasn't fooled for a minute, but she pretended to be. "Sure. Sounds like fun." She took a few steps toward the stairs, then deftly dodged to the right, around their circle—immediately spotting Landon sitting in the corner booth, holding Audrey's hand.

"It's not what it looks like, Sun," Finn murmured, placing one hand around her waist, still trying to guide her to the apartment. "She showed up here unexpected, just wanted to visit for a little while, catch up."

Sunnie stared at the table. She couldn't see Landon's face. Hell, she couldn't see more than the back of his head. But she could see his hand, holding Audrey's. And Audrey's tears. "It looks like more than that."

"Sunnie—" Yvonne started.

"You guys stay down here," Sunnie said, forcing her gaze away from the table. "I do need to change my clothes, freshen up."

*Watch something.*

"I'll be right back down, okay?" Sunnie didn't wait for a response. Instead, she headed for the stairs to the apartment, allowing herself one last peek at Landon's table.

He was still holding Audrey's hand.

"I don't know why I stayed with him," Audrey continued. "Why I kept forgiving him. He swore on Christmas it was just a mistake, too much stress over not landing a big part he'd been hoping for. I believed him. Then he gave me a black eye in January...kept me in bruises through February and March."

Landon's temper rose at the idea of any man hurting her, hurting *any* woman. He recalled the bruise on Sunnie's cheek after the mugging, then pictured Audrey with the same. "What's the man's name?" he asked darkly.

Audrey released a loud breath, part laugh, part cry. "I knew you'd ask me that. It doesn't matter. I broke things off a month or so ago, got out."

"I'm glad." He gave her hand a friendly squeeze, then released it, resisting the urge to turn around and look for Sunnie.

"I saw the video," Audrey admitted.

Landon rolled his eyes, groaning in a way he hoped would make her laugh. She was clearly still fighting some strong emotions.

It worked. This time her laugh was genuine. "It reminded me of what I'd had. What I lost."

Landon didn't like where this was headed. "Audrey—" he started, trying to head her next words off at the pass.

"I made a mistake. I never should have left you."

Landon sucked in a deep breath, preparing to tell her about Sunnie, but she kept talking.

"I love you, Landon. I want you back."


Sunnie stepped into her bedroom and closed the door, leaning against it and shutting her eyes.

"Dammit," she whispered, recalling the image of Landon holding hands with Audrey.

She'd been present for every single second of his relationship with the other woman. Heard every fucking detail, from the first date to that magical fourth kiss, from the hot sex to moving in together, his dreams of the future, the plan to buy an engagement ring, the move to New York, the year of heartbreak.

She'd walked every step of that with him.

Sunnie pushed away from the door, tugging off her scrubs, her temper flaring.

No. *No way.*

Audrey was not about to saunter back into Landon's life and take another punch at his heart. Sunnie wouldn't let her.

She pulled on some jeans, searched in the closet for a hootchie-mama shirt. She wasn't above using cleavage to help her win this war.

Sunnie peered at herself in the mirror, then decided to go for broke. She pulled down her hair, brushing it out, grateful that it held some wave. She put on the shiny pink lip gloss Landon liked, swiped on some mascara, then grabbed her phone and walked to the bed.

Moment of truth.

She clicked on YouTube and searched for the video. She considered turning off the music, as Yvonne suggested, but decided to keep it on. She loved that Faith Hill song, and music always fired her up—either to get her in the party mood or ready for battle.

This time, she kept her eyes on Landon throughout the entire thing, at his face as he knelt down to her, the way he pulled her into his arms to hug her. The fierceness when she stood up and he'd realized she'd hurt her ankle. The way he kissed her.

Even now, she could feel the passion in it.

Then they parted...

And she saw it. Saw what everyone kept talking about.

He looked at her as if she were the most beautiful woman on earth. As if she were the only person on the planet who existed. She was the center of his universe—and then she sneaked a peek at her own face, and realized the one thing no one else seemed to have noticed.

He was the center of hers too.

Then he bent over, picked her up and carried her to the police car.

Landon loved her.

He'd loved her all along.

And now it was time to tell him she felt exactly the same way.


LANDON SHOOK HIS HEAD. "AUDREY. YOU SAW THE VIDEO. You saw..."

"Sunnie?" Audrey asked.

There was a tinge of disbelief in her tone that tweaked his nerves. Why the hell was it so unbelievable that he and Sunnie could be together? Hell, even *Sunnie* had mentioned something about them being too different or a mismatch or some such shit this morning.

"Yeah," he said. "Sunnie."

Audrey leaned back, and he could see her seriously considering his face, almost as if she expected him to say he was just kidding, or maybe she thought he'd supposedly wise up now that she was throwing her hat back in the ring.

"I'm in love with her," he said, determined that she understand he was serious and what they'd had was over. He didn't want to hurt her, but he couldn't let her leave here thinking there was any chance of a future for them either. That would merely add emotional cruelty to the physical pain she'd endured since the holidays.

She nodded slowly, then smiled. "I'm happy for you."

"Really?"

Audrey laughed easily, and he recalled why he'd loved her. She was kind and understanding, and being with her had been easy. Probably too easy. They'd gone from dating to almost insta-love. There'd been no challenge and precious little passion. Just companionable...boring love.

Sunnie offered him so much more. Life with her would never be predictable or simple, but it would be fun. And they'd set the sheets on fire every single night.

"Really," Audrey said. "I'm sad to have missed my chance. I'll regret that until the day I die."

"No," Landon said, patting her hand gently. "You're too special. You're going to find the perfect, *nice*," he stressed, "guy. You'll settle down and forget all about me. You might even think back on this night and realize you'd dodged a bullet."

He didn't admit that was how *he* felt now, about her decision to move to New York rather than remain in Baltimore with him. If she had, he'd never have opened his eyes and seen Sunnie.

"From your lips," she said.

Landon lifted his pint, clinking it against her wineglass, then did what he'd wanted to do ever since sitting down.

He looked over his shoulder for Sunnie.

Sunnie emerged from the apartment, back into the pub, and glanced in Landon's direction. He and Audrey were still talking, then they clinked glasses. She was smiling.

Sunnie didn't want to think about what that smile might mean.

She considered walking right over to their table, but paused briefly, trying to figure out what she would say. She'd royally screwed up this morning. It was going to take some finesse to get him away from Audrey so she could fix that.

Glancing around the pub, she realized Pop Pop was at the bar —and he was looking at her.

She decided to go that direction first. Pop Pop gave great pep talks.

"Hey, Pop Pop," she said, claiming the stool next to him.

He smiled at her. "You finally watched the video."

She nodded. "Yeah."

"And?"

"And Landon loves me. And I love him. And I really fucking hate that he's talking to Audrey."

"Language," Pop Pop said, something she'd heard no less than a million times from him whenever she or Finn or Mom cussed.

She issued the obligatory "Sorry," then continued, "Why do you think she's here?"

"If she's intelligent, and I believe she is, I'd say she's come to ask Landon to take her back. I think she's regretting letting him go to begin with."

Sunnie sighed. "Yeah. That's what I think too."

"So, what are you going to do about it?"

"He's *mine*. I'm going over there and getting him."

Pop Pop lifted his pint glass. "That's my girl. So what are you still doing over here?"

"I need advice."

"Lass, it sounds to me like you've made up your mind."

"Oh, not about that. I'm definitely staking my Landon claim. The question is…how? What do you think? Richard Gere style?"

Pop Pop chuckled. He was a sucker for a romantic comedy, a love he'd passed on to his granddaughters. Sunnie couldn't count how many afternoons she'd spent with him—either in the living room or at the theater—watching everyone from Tom Hanks to Meg Ryan to Julia Roberts fall head over heels in love.

"I'm not sure where you'd find a limo and bouquet of roses at this time of night," Pop Pop said.

"Good point. Of course, there's always the *Officer and a Gentleman* route. I could go over there, pick him up and carry him out of here."

Pop Pop pretended to consider her upper-body strength, then shook his head. "No. I think you and Landon have already had that moment."

She gave him a confused look, until he said, "The night of the mugging. Remember? It's probably too soon in your relationship to start rehashing the big endings."

Sunnie laughed. "Excellent point. So…should I ask him to meet me on top of the Empire State Building, flash cue cards at him like in *Love Actually*, sing 'Grow Old with You' on a plane, tell him no one puts baby in a corner, or that he had me at hello?"

"You could just tell him you love him."

Sunnie turned around at his voice, surprised to see Landon standing behind her. She glanced over his shoulder.

"She's gone," Landon said. "So..."

Sunnie pressed her lips together, trying not to laugh at his far-too-happy grin. "So, just saying it feels pretty lame, babe. It lacks a certain..."

"Romance?"

She sighed. "Yeah."

"Don't you think the beginning was already pretty romantic?"

She considered that. "Going viral was cool. And I do like Faith Hill."

Landon narrowed his eyes. "Those were the parts you found romantic?"

Sunnie slid off the stool and stepped closer. "Well, the kiss was pretty awesome. And when you carried me to—"

Sunnie didn't get the chance to finish her sentence when Landon tugged her toward him and gave her another one of those earth-shattering kisses.

"Still trying to shut me up?" she joked.

"Yes." He kissed her again.

She wrapped her hands around his neck as he cupped her face between his hands. The kiss might have lasted longer if they weren't interrupted.

"Jesus. Are you two still playing that damn game?"

She and Landon turned to face her father.

Sunnie giggled as Landon cleared his throat. Finn was standing directly behind their dad, arms crossed, grinning.

"Oh for pity's sake, sugar. You know they were never pretending." Mom pushed her way by Dad, reaching for Landon to pull him in for a hug.

Dad smirked. "Finally admitting it, Sunnie?"

She nodded.

"I knew it was going to take a special guy to get my head-strong girl to fall in love."

Sunnie rolled her eyes when Dad shook Landon's hand, acting like he'd just saved half a dozen kids from a fire.

"No more pretending?" Dad asked.

"No, sir," Landon said.

"I think it's perfect," her mom sighed.

Dad looked from her to Landon, then back at her. "Landon, huh?" he asked with a grin.

"Oh my God. Seriously, you two. Can we please not make this into a big thing? Landon and I are just dating."

Landon wrapped his arm around her waist. "She's head over heels for me. I'm already planning our entire future in my head."

Dad laughed. "Glad to hear it. About time you both took your heads out of your asses and realized what was right in front of you."

"Too far," Sunnie mumbled. "Everyone is going *way* too far."

Finn couldn't resist jumping in to tease her. "Collins curse claims another victim."

Dad slapped Finn on the shoulder. "Maybe you'll be next."

Finn's eyes widened, and Sunnie was delighted when the joke was suddenly on him. "Why would you even *say* that? It's like daring the universe!"

Mom and Dad walked away laughing as Sunnie turned to face Landon, her eyes narrowed.

"Oh man. I think we all managed to bring on another freak-out," Finn muttered.

Landon never took his eyes off her as he spoke to her brother. "Twenty bucks, Finn, if you and Miguel guard the exits and keep her from leaving."

"Each?" Finn clarified.

"Each."

Finn jerked his head toward Miguel, who was already moving into position. "I'll cover the pub. You take Sunday's Side," Miguel said.

Sunnie shook her head. "Planning our entire future? Like *forever* future?"

He nodded. "Yep."

"Is this how slow you're planning to take things?"

"Yep."

"You're going to have to cough up that forty bucks," Sunnie said. "Because I'm going through those doors in about ten seconds."

Landon reached out, his hands gripping her waist as he frowned. "Sunnie."

"I have to. I promised Yvonne we'd spend the night at your place. She'd like to get some sleep tonight."

Landon laughed and reached for his wallet. "Let's go."

He grasped her hand, slipped Miguel a twenty, grumbled when the man kept it, then led her to his car.

She was touched when he opened the passenger door for her. "Quite the gentleman."

Landon snuck a quick kiss, then his gaze slid lower. "I like your shirt."

Sunnie kissed his jaw. "I knew you would."

"Using the girls to get my attention?"

"Worked, didn't it?"

He nodded, then ran his finger over her cleavage. "Oh yeah."

They got into the car.

"So...Audrey," she said, when he pulled onto the road.

"Yeah. She had a rough year in New York."

"And she came back to tell you that?"

Landon glanced over at her. "She came to say she wanted me back."

"What did *you* say?"

He laughed loudly. "I'm sitting in the car with *you* at the moment, so I'll let you puzzle that one out."

Sunnie punched his arm. "Smart-ass."

"No more freaking out?"

She shook her head. "I'm sorry about this morning. Really sorry."

He accepted her apology with nothing more than a pleased

smile that warmed her heart. "I know this is all new for you, Sunnie. Committed relationships. We can take it slow."

"Thanks."

"Besides, you recovered from your freak-out pretty quick."

"Yvonne and Kelli helped me see the error of my ways. So did the video."

He stopped at a traffic light. "You watched it again?"

She nodded. "You knew then, didn't you?"

"Sunshine, I'm pretty sure I knew on April Fools. That second kiss just sealed the deal."

"So what you're *really* saying is, I beat Audrey by three kisses."

He reached over and ruffled her hair, something he'd been doing since they were kids. She shoved his hands away, grinning.

"Wanna know a secret?" she asked.

"Sure."

"I knew at April Fools too."

The light turned green so he started driving again. "Is that right?"

"Problem is, I didn't realize that's what it was."

"You realize you still haven't said the words," Landon pointed out.

"Neither have you."

Before he could reply to that, they were at his place. "Sunnie…" He leaned close to her as he turned off the car.

She twisted in her seat and leaned forward as well, expecting him to tell her how he felt.

"When we get upstairs, I'm going to punish you for freaking out. Then I'm going to strip you naked and do very dirty things to you."

Old Sunnie would have been ridiculously turned on by that prospect.

New Sunnie wanted those damn three little words.

Then she reared back, something he'd said sinking in. "Punish me?"

Landon opened the door, then came around, taking her hand as she got out too. He wrapped his arm around her waist as they walked into his building, drawing her close enough that he could whisper in her ear.

"I'm going to push those sexy jeans down to your ankles, bend you over my bed, and spank your cute little ass until you promise to never again run out on me in the middle of a fight. Especially one where I'm naked and hard."

Sunnie, because she was contrary, ran her hand along the front of his jeans. "Bet that hurt."

He narrowed his eyes, then pressed her hand more firmly against him, letting her know he was right back to the same place he'd been this morning when she left. "You have no idea. Hence the spanking."

She laughed as they got into the elevator, the sound fading when he didn't even crack a smile. "You're joking about that, right?"

He shook his head. "Not even a little bit. Besides, I spanked you last night."

"Those were swats in the heat of the moment," she sputtered. "You can't spank me like I'm some badly behaved child!"

"Of course I can. And believe me, the way I do it won't make you feel like a kid." He pressed her against the wall of the elevator, kissing her cheek, his breath hot in her ear when he said, "If I do it right, you'll have your first orgasm that way."

The elevator doors opened and Sunnie stumbled to his apartment, feeling drunk even though she'd only had a couple margaritas—and that had been two hours earlier.

Once they were inside, Landon grabbed her hand, dragging her to his bedroom at record speed as she giggled.

"Landon, it's a marathon, babe. Not a sprint."

He turned toward her once they were in his room, hands on his hips. "Pants off."

Sunnie unfastened her jeans, sliding the zipper down slowly. Then she began to shimmy out of the denim, letting it slip over her hips one little inch at a time, grinning as she did so. She left her panties in place. Her sensual, slow striptease was driving him crazy.

Landon watched her through narrowed, hungry eyes. "Keep it up, Sunshine. It's only adding to your punishment."

She rolled her eyes—which turned out to be his breaking point.

"That's it."

Landon strode over, picked her up and tossed her onto her back on his bed. She barely had time to push up on her elbows before he had her shoes, jeans and panties tugged off.

"Give a girl a chance," she protested, but Landon wasn't in a patient mood. That point was driven home when he gripped one of her arms and flipped her to her stomach.

Sunnie tried to lift up, to crawl away, but Landon bent over her, his chest pressed to her back.

"Hold still," he warned her.

Sunnie had never been particularly good at doing as she was told. Not that Landon was giving her much choice. The man was wicked strong. He stood again, one hand resting in the center of her back, holding her in place.

Then he spanked her ass, three rapid-fire and hard swats.

"Ow!"

He repeated the action, and she tried once more to move away.

"Open your legs."

Sunnie stilled.

"Sunnie," he murmured, his voice almost a purr.

She parted her thighs, and he ran his fingers along her slit, from clit to ass.

"Oh God," she whispered. "Yes."

She lifted her hips toward him, but Landon pulled his fingers away, methodically spanking her a half dozen more times. Her ass felt like it was on fire, but it wasn't exactly painful. It was... Sunnie struggled to figure it out.

It was something else entirely.

Something hot and sexy.

He alternated every spank with sexy strokes, playing with her clit, toying with her ass.

"Inside me," she begged. "Put your fingers inside me."

Her request earned her three more swats, these on her upper thighs.

"Dammit, Landon!" she cried when, once more, he added pressure to her clit while ignoring her empty, clenching pussy. "I can't take it. I need—"

"Thought it was a marathon."

She shot him a looks-could-kill glare over her shoulder, but it only made him laugh. "I'm going to tell my dad and Finn you spanked me. I'm pretty sure they'll beat you up for that."

He caressed her sore bottom. "I'm pretty sure they won't."

She sighed. "I need—" she started again.

"I know what you need, Sunshine."

Finally, he pressed two fingers inside her, and she felt as if she could cry with relief.

"You're so wet," he murmured. "Wet and hot and tight."

She pressed her forehead to the mattress, her hips moving toward him practically of their own volition. She was going to explode, splinter apart into a million shining pieces.

Landon moved his fingers in and out as slowly as she'd stripped off her jeans, the pace driving her insane.

"Faster," she urged.

He didn't comply.

"Harder," she tried.

Again, he kept up the same gentle, slow motion. Sunnie tried to take matters into her own hands, attempting to get some sort of traction on the mattress so she could set the pace she desired. Landon's hand on her back prevented that.

"Please," she whispered, her inner muscles quivering, her heart racing. She was close, but he wasn't giving her enough to push her over.

"Tell me what you want."

"You. I want *you*."

"Promise you won't run from me again, Sunnie. I can't take another day like today."

She stopped trying to reach for more. Instead, she lifted her head, looked over her shoulder, captured his gaze and nodded. "I'm not running anymore, Landon. I'm exactly where I want to be."

He leaned toward her, pressing a kiss to her shoulder.

Then he gave her everything she wanted. He'd promised her first orgasm would come from the punishment, and he hadn't lied. With *her* promise still hovering in the air, he let loose, thrusting three fingers inside her, deep and hard, setting a fast pace that had her head spinning.

She came with a loud cry, calling out his name, but Landon didn't relent, didn't stop.

The hand on her back slid upwards, his fingers wrapping themselves in her hair. He clenched his fist, tugging just shy of real pain.

She groaned.

"Come again," he demanded. "One more time, and then we're going to get serious."

She would have laughed at that comment—what the fuck was *this* if not serious?—but there wasn't a bit of spare breath in her body.

There was no way she could come again so quickly.

But she should have known better. Landon's hand tightened in her hair as he withdrew his fingers, sliding one wet digit all the way into her ass.

She trembled roughly. "Holy. Shit. *Please*."

"Keep begging me, Sunnie. I like it."

Every word came out alone, punctuated with a harsh breath. Sunnie felt like she'd actually run that damn marathon. "Please. God. Please. I. Need..."

Her pussy clenched when his fingers returned, sending her

into orbit once more. She pressed her legs together when his fingers finally slipped away.

Sunnie was vaguely aware of him moving around behind her. She assumed he was getting undressed. She would have liked to watch the show, but he'd set her on fire and reduced her to ash. She couldn't move, not even to open her eyes.

She jumped slightly when he lightly stroked her ass.

"Okay, babe?" he asked.

"Not sure, but I think I had an out-of-body experience," she murmured.

He chuckled as he sat on the mattress next to her, running his fingers gently over her bare bottom, reminding her of the spanking. She considered what she could do to encourage him to spank her again one night...or, well...every night.

"I hope you learned your lesson," he said, adopting a stern voice.

Sunnie giggled. "Um. Well. Hate to break it to you, but..."

"But?" he prompted.

She turned her face toward him, forcing her eyes open. "I was actually just wondering what I could do to make you spank me again."

He shook his head. "I wouldn't worry about that too much. You're an accomplished pain in the ass, remember?"

She pushed herself to her back, then sat up, wincing slightly at the pressure on her bottom. "Ouch. Maybe I've changed my mind on the spanking."

"You haven't," he said, as he reached for the hem of her shirt, pulling it off in one swoop. Then with skilled fingers, he rid her of her bra.

She lay down on her back, parting her legs, loving how natural it felt when he turned toward her, caging her beneath him.

"How did we only just now find each other?" she whispered. "You were always there. Why didn't I see you?"

He kissed her softly, the head of his cock at her opening. "I don't know, but we're here now."

"I love you," she said, her heart overflowing with the emotion.

He smiled and kissed her again. "You said it first," he teased.

Sunnie narrowed her eyes. "And you better say it ba—"

"I love you too. So much it hurts."

She'd never understood that saying until now, with him. Now she got it, realized she was filled to the brim with the emotion, so full of love, she felt as if she couldn't contain it all, as if she'd come apart at the seams.

Landon kissed her one more time, then slowly slid inside, not stopping until he was buried deep. He took her slowly at first, as they kissed, touched, stroked each other.

Then, their marathon turned to a sprint, both of them too close to go slow. His thrusts grew harder.

"God, Sunshine," he said at last. "So close."

She closed her eyes, throwing her head back. "Already. There!"

Sunnie came again, and Landon followed her over.

It was ecstasy. Bliss.

Sweet oblivion.

Landon fell to her side, breathing heavy. "I think you should move in with me."

Sunnie laughed. "So much for taking it slow."

EPILOGUE

"You and Landon didn't have to drive me home, lass." Pop Pop walked into his room at her parents' house and switched on the lamp. He'd moved in with her family over a decade earlier, when Sunnie was a teenager. She'd always loved her home, loved her family, but when Pop Pop moved in, it was as if all the magic and fun was amplified. She wasn't sure how she would have made it through high school without him there in the house.

"Oh, I know, but we were ready to leave, and you and I both know Mom and Bubbles aren't leaving that dance floor until they're kicked out."

Sunnie's cousin Caitlyn had married her Prince Charming, Lucas Whiting, tonight in a beautiful September wedding. Landon had been her date for the event. Hell, he'd been her date for everything since June.

"Well, you certainly didn't need to leave him waiting in the living room. I don't need to be put to bed like a toddler," Pop Pop insisted.

"I know that. I just wanted to steal a few minutes alone to tell you something."

Pop Pop glanced at her curiously, then sat down in his

favorite chair, patting the cushion of the one next to him. Dad and Finn had built an extension onto the house, creating a father-in-law suite, so to speak, before Pop Pop moved in. It was just one big bedroom with a nice-sized seating area, complete with his own big-screen TV.

Pop Pop called it his bachelor pad, claiming he liked having somewhere to charm his lady friends. The funny part was, Pop Pop had never entertained anyone here besides the family. He'd lost his heart to Sunday a million years ago, and he'd never looked at another woman since.

"Oh," Pop Pop said, clearly excited. "A secret?"

"Sort of, but not really. I'll be screaming this from the rafters tomorrow. Landon and I agreed to keep it quiet until then. Today was Caitlyn's day. And maybe Fergus's."

Her cousin Fergus had returned from two tours in the military, making it back to Baltimore halfway through the reception. Sunnie was thrilled he was home to stay, and he'd been delighted to hear that she and Landon were a couple.

"It is nice to have that boy home for good."

Sunnie knew Pop Pop had worried about Fergus the entire time he'd been stationed in the Middle East. "I've missed him too."

"Caitlyn's wedding was just beautiful." Pop Pop wiped away a tear. "I never dreamed I'd have a chance to see so many of my dear grandchildren meet their soul mates and fall in love. I've lived a blessed life indeed."

She took his hand and squeezed it affectionately, purposely ignoring that it felt thinner, frailer. Sunnie knew in her heart Pop Pop wouldn't live forever, but damn if she wouldn't try to will it so. There was no reason he couldn't pull a Dumbledore and keep kicking until about a hundred and fifty or so.

"That's actually my secret." Sunnie lifted her other hand, revealing the engagement ring Landon had put on her finger only a couple hours earlier. He'd pulled her out onto the balcony of the hotel ballroom, gotten down on one knee and proposed.

She'd been shocked and thrilled...but she'd playfully chastised him for moving so damn fast. Again.

She'd moved in with him in June, after making him promise he would be okay with simply shacking up together for a year or two. He'd broken that vow tonight. But the ring was gorgeous, so she forgave him instantly.

"Landon proposed, and I said yes! He's promised it can be a long engagement, but you know him. Apparently a long time to him is two months."

There was a knock at the door, and Landon peeked his head in. "Can I come in now?"

"You were listening outside the whole time, weren't you?" she accused.

Landon shrugged, not bothering to deny it.

"Come in here, son. Sunnie was just telling me the big news."

Sunnie looked at Pop Pop and rolled her eyes. "He's incorrigible, Pop Pop. If he'd had his way, we would have announced the engagement at the wedding three seconds after I said yes."

"I thought you were going to wait to propose," Pop Pop said to Landon, who grinned sheepishly.

"Wait?" Sunnie looked at her grandfather. "You *knew* he was going to ask me to marry him?"

"He asked your father and me for our blessing last week. Said he was going to pop the question over Thanksgiving."

"Weddings get to me," Landon said unapologetically.

"He cried," Sunnie said.

"I told you, Sunshine, I got something in my eye," Landon insisted.

"Just as Caitlyn was walking down the aisle?" she persisted.

"I got something in my eye at that point too," Pop Pop admitted.

"You really asked for their blessing?" Sunnie asked. "Isn't that kind of old-fashioned?"

"Don't give him a hard time for that, lass," Pop Pop chastised. "That was for your father and me. A very respectful thing to do."

She felt warm inside when Pop Pop looked at Landon with genuine fondness. Her grandfather's blessing meant the world to her. And given Landon's smile, it was clear he felt the same way.

"So, should I clear my schedule for a Christmas wedding?" Pop Pop joked.

"Only if I can't convince her to marry me over Thanksgiving," Landon said, the two men laughing as Sunnie rolled her eyes.

"That's not a long engagement," she said.

Landon wrapped his arm around her, kissing her on the cheek. "Thanksgiving is a lifetime away."

"It was the same way with your father, lass. The second Riley let him know she was ready to settle down in marriage, he dragged her off to the Elvis Chapel and made it official."

"Mom tells it a little differently. Says she was drunk and doesn't remember the wedding at all."

"Perhaps not the first one," Pop Pop said with a chuckle. "But it only took him a few days to convince her to repeat those vows again...sober."

Landon shook his head, even though he'd heard the story countless times before. "Only in your family, Sunnie."

"Your family now too, Landon," Pop Pop reminded him. "Looks like you managed to get your wish. Let me show you both something."

Pop Pop had a wall of photographs, each frame holding a picture of one of his children or grandchildren. Every member of the family was represented. He pointed to Sunnie's spot...and she laughed when she saw her new photo.

"How on earth?" she asked.

"Your friend Miguel helped me with that," Pop Pop confessed. "Said he could take a picture from the video—I had no idea that was possible! Then he did some sort of trick with his computer where he brightened it up. Looks good, doesn't it?"

Pop Pop had gotten Miguel to freeze-frame that perfect moment, right after their viral kiss, when Landon looked at her as if she hung the moon.

"Sunnie," Landon said, studying it closely. "Your face."

No one had ever mentioned the way she was looking at him before now. It was always *his* expression that was remarked on.

"That's why I asked for the photo, son," Pop Pop said. "See how she's looking at you?"

Sunnie crossed her arms, pretending to be annoyed with her fiancé. "So what you're saying is...even though you watched that video a thousand times, you were only looking at yourself? Typical," she teased.

Landon wrapped his arm around her waist, kissing her on the cheek. "Couldn't help it. My ass looks damn fine in that video."

Pop Pop chuckled. "In those romantic movies, they always have to wait until the end for their happily ever after. It seems to me the two of you found it right at the beginning."

Sunnie kissed her grandfather on the cheek. "You're as mushy-gushy as Landon."

"You kept your promise to me, lass. Found the man who loves you for the sunshine and happiness you bring. And, Landon," Pop Pop said, "Sunnie found a way to give you *your* wish as well. You're officially a Collins now. It's the perfect ending."

I HOPE YOU ENJOYED THIS FIRST BOOK IN THE WILDER IRISH series. Why not dive all the way in? The next book, Wild Fire, is available now.

HAVE YOU READ THE ENTIRE WILDER IRISH SERIES? ALL THE books are standalone, so they can be read in any order. Be sure to check out all of them!

Wild Passion

Wild Desire
Wild Devotion
Wild at Heart
Wild Temptation
Wild Kisses
Wild Fire
Wild Spirit
Wild Side
Wild Night
Wild Embrace
Wild Dreams
Wild Chance

FANS OF WILD IRISH AND FACEBOOK! THERE'S A GROUP FOR you. Come join the Wild Irish Facebook group for sneak peaks, cover reveals, contests and more! Join now.

BE SURE TO JOIN MY NEWSLETTER FOR A **FREE** WILDER IRISH short story, One Wild Night.

TURN THE PAGE TO READ AN EXCERPT FROM WILD FIRE, available now.

# WILD FIRE

"Truth or dare?" she whispered.

He glanced up at her, then slowly lowered her shirt, shifting away.

"Truth," he chose again.

She snickered lightly. "Coward."

Fergus shook his head. "Wise."

Aubrey returned to the couch, thinking about what she wanted to ask. The main question she wanted an answer to slipped out before she could think better of it. "Since you don't have a serious girlfriend, I'm curious. When was the last time you had sex?"

Fergus, true to character, never blinked twice. "August."

"It's the beginning of June now. That was a long time ago. Who was she?"

"My first response wasn't a yes or no."

She grinned. "But it was a one-word answer. Those always allow for follow-up questions."

Fergus stood, coming to sit next to her on the couch. "Now I *know* you're cheating. But I also know you'll keep asking until you get your response, so in the interest of moving the game along...her name was Jeanne. She and I went through basic training together, which was where we first hooked up. Our military paths diverged from there, but whenever we ran into each other, we got together. We were compatible lovers."

Aubrey crinkled her nose. "Compatible sounds boring," she teased.

Fergus didn't laugh, but she could tell he didn't take offense either. "Compatible in this case means she would let me handcuff her wrists together, bend her over the nearest flat surface, spank her ass and fuck her from behind."

Aubrey sucked in a deep breath, perfectly aware that Fergus heard her gasp.

"Oh," she said. If every inch of her being wasn't focused on the forceful clenching of her pussy, she might have tried for more words. She couldn't spare the energy. Instead, she was wondering if, one, she had time to pay a visit to her vibrator, and two, if she did, would Fergus hear her and—please God—join her in her bedroom?

"In case you haven't noticed, I prefer to be in control—in and out of the bedroom."

She wished she had the strength to smile, but every single thing he said merely turned her on more. She could understand his desire for power. Aubrey had spent too much of her adult life struggling to hold on to control. It was exhausting, but with no one she could trust to rely on, she'd had no choice. The idea of giving Fergus control over her—even if it was just her body in the bedroom—sounded like heaven.

Aubrey swallowed heavily, fighting to shake free of whatever spell he'd cast on her. "I don't need anyone to con—"

He chuckled. "*You* need it most of all."

Their gazes were locked, neither of them denying the truth of what he'd just said. She could scoff, dismiss it as bullshit, but he'd know she was lying.

Then what would he do?

*Punish me.*

The thought of Fergus punishing her every time she behaved

like a brat shook her to the core...and made her long for something she'd never dreamed of.

"Truth or dare," Fergus murmured. It figured he'd get into the game just as she was struggling to recall her own name.

"Truth," she said, before recalling that wasn't what she wanted. "I mean da—"

"No. Rules state you have to stick with your first choice."

She laughed, albeit weakly, when Fergus decided to do a little cheating of his own. "Fine."

"What are your hard limits?"

Aubrey opened her mouth, but no sound came out. Were they talking about having sex? Was he propositioning her, or was this still part of the game?

When the silence stretched too long, Fergus broke it. "Do you understand the question?"

She nodded. "I...can't...think of any." It probably didn't help that her experience with the type of sex play he was discussing was limited to...none.

Suddenly, all she could see was Fergus, binding her to the bed, blindfolding her, spanking her, taking parts of her that had never been touched before.

This was the most sexually charged moment of her life, and Fergus hadn't even kissed her, hadn't touched her except for that soft brushing stroke on her shoulder. God, all he'd done was talk to her, plant seeds, draw pictures. He should be the songwriter, not her.

"Do you want to hear mine?" he asked.

"Yes."

"I don't whip women with anything other than my hand. I don't humiliate them. And I don't share."

She realized her lack of knowledge had impacted her hard limits response. "I don't think I know enough to fully answer your question."

"I'm aware of that."

She didn't like the dismissive tone in his voice. It suggested that he didn't consider her the type of woman he could dominate in the bedroom.

"Truth or dare," she countered before he could end the game and walk away.

"Dare."

"Kiss me."

He shook his head even before she'd finished issuing the dare. "No. The game stops here."

"Why?"

"You know why."

Aubrey didn't want to admit that she did. If they kissed, it wouldn't stop there. It would carry over to her bedroom, where she'd let him test every single one of those hard limits he was curious about. And while her body was screaming out for that, her chest started to grow tight, fear creeping in.

He reached over and cupped her cheek, the sexy, brooding man she'd been playing the game with vanishing, replaced by safe, friendly Fergus again. "The things I ask of my lovers require absolute trust, Aubrey."

Aubrey hated that fucking word. "I can't...give you...that."

He smiled kindly, and she thought maybe even sadly. "I know."

WILD FIRE IS OUT NOW.

# ABOUT THE AUTHOR

Virginia native Mari Carr is a New York Times and USA TODAY bestseller of contemporary romance novels. With over two million copies of her books sold, Mari was the winner of the Romance Writers of America's Passionate Plume award for her novella, Erotic Research. She has over a hundred published works, including her popular Wild Irish and Compass books, along with the Trinity Masters/Masters Admiralty series she writes with Lila Dubois.

*Find Mari Carr on the web at*
www.maricarr.com
mari@maricarr.com